EXILE

by

AL SARRANTONIO

It is the end of the 25th century. Human civilization has expanded into the Four Worlds of Earth, Mars, Titan, and Pluto. Recent progress in terraforming promises to turn Venus into the Fifth. But for Prime Cornelian, usurper of Martian rule, there will be no rest until all planets bow before him. With the blood of treason and treachery on his hand, he is rekindling the ancient savagery for which Martians were once feared . . . and supplementing it with a new secret weapon of awesome power.

Dalin Shar, King of Earth, must flee his besieged palace as his government falls to Martian intrigue. Exiled far from home, at the mercy of strangers he barely trusts, the king struggles to stay alive long enough to gather rebel forces. . . .

> "Sarrantonio has packed more into one book than George Lucas did in his *Star Wars* trilogy! *Exile* is a must read for anyone wanting to be swept away to worlds where wonder is the byword."
> —George W. Proctor, author of *Shadowrun*

> "One of the most striking things about Sarrantonio's work is his *originality*."
> —Thomas F. Monteleone, author of *The Resurrectionist*

JOURNEY

THE FIVE WORLDS SAGA

Al Sarrantonio

A ROC BOOK

ROC
Published by the Penguin Group
Penguin Books USA Inc., 375 Hudson Street,
New York, New York 10014, U.S.A.
Penguin Books Ltd, 27 Wrights Lane,
London W8 5TZ, England
Penguin Books Australia Ltd, Ringwood,
Victoria, Australia
Penguin Books Canada Ltd, 10 Alcorn Avenue,
Toronto, Ontario, Canada M4V 3B2
Penguin Books (N.Z.) Ltd, 182–190 Wairau Road,
Auckland 10, New Zealand

Penguin Books Ltd, Registered Offices:
Harmondsworth, Middlesex, England

First published by Roc, an imprint of Dutton Signet,
a division of Penguin Books USA Inc.

First Printing, March, 1997
10 9 8 7 6 5 4 3 2 1

Cover art by Donato

 REGISTERED TRADEMARK—MARCA REGISTRADA

Printed in the United States of America

BOOKS ARE AVAILABLE AT QUANTITY DISCOUNTS WHEN USED TO PROMOTE
PRODUCTS OR SERVICES. FOR INFORMATION PLEASE WRITE TO PREMIUM MAR-
KETING DIVISION, PENGUIN BOOKS USA INC., 375 HUDSON STREET, NEW
YORK, NEW YORK 10014.

For Tom Disch,
Mentor:
With Long Overdue Thanks.

1

Teacher said, "The Carthaginians, an ancient Earth race, were known primarily for their migratory abilities. Within their own small sphere . . ."

For the fiftieth time this morning, Visid Sneaden's eyes wandered from the holographic Screen image of the robed instructor to the room's floor-to-ceiling window. Outside, red dust was kicking up; it had been threatening to storm since sunrise. The pink sky had visibly darkened, and at the horizon what looked like the cone of a tornado had appeared briefly, toying with the rim of Wells Crater. But so far, the Screen had not blanked and they had not been sent home.

Visid prayed for release; had prayed all week. She was weary of lessons, wearied most of all by their increased intensity. Instruction was bad enough, but the recent increase in daily school hours from nine to eleven had incurred in Visid, and in her classmates, she supposed, a condition close to dust blindness. So much information—most of it tedious—and so little time to digest it. It was said that there was a reason; was whispered in the dormitories, in the lowest tones, that the reason was a drastic one: that they were to be returned to Venus within the month. Visid didn't believe this: there had been such rumors before.

So instead she prayed for . . . dust storms.

And still the day dragged on, without release. At lunchtime, which had recently been cut in half, Visid stayed, as usual, by herself. A cluster of other students sat by the Screen, listening to Doctrine lectures; but since it was not mandatory now, Visid chose to abstain. She knew that her aloofness, and especially her reluctance to indulge in extra Doctrine, had been duly noted; she knew that somewhere, someone was compiling her minor rebellions into a compact evidential file, no doubt entered on a data card, and that sooner or later she would be interviewed about it.

But she didn't care, even though she was not rebellious at all.

She was . . . bored.

The lessons, which were thorough but repetitive, had ceased to be of interest to her months ago. The other students around her, even those she had nominally made friends with, such as Amie, didn't seem to notice that they were being fed the same diet day after day, only with different seasonings. In Visid's mind, once the facts had been absorbed, she found the outer coating with which they were presented to be of no interest or use. The occasional new tidbit of fact she was able to glean from the mountain of

canon (no one dared say propaganda) she was fed
was not enough to sustain her interest.

And so her mind wandered.

And she prayed for dust storms.

After lunch came Theory, and after that came Fact
(indistinguishable from Doctrine) and then Culture
(again indistinguishable from Doctrine). For a few
moments, her attention was drawn from the window
to the Screen during today's Culture lesson, which
concerned Titan. The teacher, a gaunt, almost sickly-
looking man with light Martian features, was full of
zeal, which usually produced ennui in Visid. But in
the midst of his harangue about the evils of Titanians, and especially the depraved mind and ances-
try of Wrath-Pei, the present Titanian despot and
former pirate, whose ouster from Mars (now cele-
brated as a Martian holiday) where he had once
"fouled the atmosphere of the already corrupt Senate, to the point where his poison had so infected his
fellow Martians that only the High Leader himself,
then a humble servant of the people known only as
Prime Cornelian, was able to free Mars of the base
Wrath-Pei himself and then, with the heroic act of a
true patriot and lover of Mars, to free the planet of
the vile and contemptible institution the Martian Senate, which was Wrath-Pei's base for his loathsome
operations, including but not confined to child prosti-
tution, the eating of human flesh, the boiling of preg-
nant mothers alive," etc., etc.—in the midst of this
mishmash, Visid learned something new.

It was long known to Martian schoolchildren and their Venusian expatriate cousins, that Wrath-Pei confined himself to the "stench-filled environs of Titan itself; Titan: whose atmosphere was unbreathable to any but corrupt beings, whose poison-filled oceans made those of Earth look paradisaic, whose surface was warmed by no natural sun but by an infernal internal heat source, which also produced an artificially enhanced gravity similar to that of the penal planet Pluto; whose perpetual night (so appropriate) was only broken by unnatural lights, and where the warming Sun would shine but weakly; and whose hell-darkened sky, nearly as black as the rogue exile planet Pluto's, was dominated not by Sol but by devilish Saturn." Never in any lesson in Ethics, Doctrine, History, Science, Politics, Theory, Fact, or Religion (where the satanic qualities of Titan's dominant religion, Moral Guidance, were more than emphasized) had Visid ever heard a single utterance even hinting that the despised Wrath-Pei was anywhere other than his own planet. It was not necessary for Martian mothers to scare their children with threats of Wrath-Pei, because the baby-eater and pirate would never dare come near Mars to begin with.

But today, there was a slip—and new information.

Deep into the usual blather, the teacher suddenly gave a hitch in his speech, as if his eyes had hit unfamiliar words on his 'prompter, and then he continued, "And so, dear students, when the vile corrupter, Wrath-Pei, is turned back to his nest, driven back down into the befouled Titanian muck from which he seeks to rise . . ."

Visid's eyes were immediately glued to the Screen; she waited for more, but the teacher immediately lapsed into the familiar sermon: "Where Titanian children, deprived of every happiness, unlike we on Mars, thanks to the benificent High Leader . . ."

And so on, and so on.

Visid, still startled by the nugget of new information which had tickled her ears, looked quickly around to see if anyone else had noticed.

All eyes were glued to the Screen, all faces, including that of Visid's friend Amie, painted with rapt stupor.

Was she the only one who noticed—or cared?

She stared raptly at the Screen for a while herself, waiting for new thoughts to come from the ill-looking Martian teacher, but nothing more was forthcoming.

Before long, Culture gave way to Religion, and once again Visid's eyes were drawn to the window, where red dust danced in a pink sky outside.

It was after classes had finally ended, without deliverance from the threatening dust storm, which had abated, that Visid was abruptly faced with the summons she knew would one day come.

As the students rose after the Religion teacher's lecture ended, the Screen blanked and then brightened once more, showing a Martian monitor, head shaved, stern.

"Visid Sneaden, remain," the monitor said, eyes unblinking.

The Screen went blank again.

Visid looked to Amie; their eyes briefly locked before Amie looked away; but as her friend filed past her she gripped Visid's hand briefly and whispered, "Be good."

Before Visid could answer, her friend had moved on, and soon Visid was left alone in the classroom.

The door slid open, revealing an attendant.

The robot, a lower, undressed model, said, "Follow."

With no alternative, Visid trailed the silver machine out of the classroom and into unfamiliar territory.

Her usual path, with all the other students, was right hallway, down stairs, short corridor, up stairs, out into waiting transport to dormitories.

Today she was taken left hallway.

Instantly, her curiosity and interest was awakened.

Pink sandstone soon gave way, after a short stairway down and through a windowless door to steel walls. Unopened doors lined both sides. Behind one Visid heard faint moaning, which sounded machine-like.

The untalking attendant led her onward.

Another hallway left, and then the first door stood open.

The robot stood outside and indicated that Visid should enter ahead of it.

As she passed she let her hand brush against the attendant's chromed chest; its eyes briefly widened.

Inside a steel room was a chair, a desk, a larger chair behind it.

"Sit," the attendant said.

Visid did so; when she turned to look at the attendant, it was gone and the door had slid closed.

Another door, behind the larger chair, slid open, and the Culture teacher, gaunt and even more sickly-looking in person, entered and sat down. He bore a hand viewer, which he placed on the desk. His colors were very pale, his forehead higher than it looked on Screen and his eyes more tired and lifeless.

"You're—" Visid began.

"I have many duties," the teacher began. "One of them is to instruct."

The teacher activated the hand viewer and sat studying it. When Visid opened her mouth to speak, he held up his hand for silence.

"Let me complete what I'm doing," he said tonelessly.

Visid studied the walls, which were without ornament; the floor, which was rugless; the desk, which seemed of a piece with the rest of the room, as if it had grown like a mushroom out of steel.

"Don't fidget," the teacher said.

Visid tried to sit still, without success.

"You have not responded to any instruction," the teacher said, putting the viewer down on the desk and deactivating it.

"I'm bored."

"So it would seem. But not so bored as to show reaction at new information today."

Visid said nothing.

"You are extremely bright," Teacher went on, but his voice was still toneless. "You are unresponsive to indoctrination."

Visid sat motionless, not knowing how to act.

"And yet your aptitude for sciences is remarkable."

"My father was an engineer."

"Yes. A Venusian traitor."

"I was nine when he was killed."

"And you are twelve now. The point?"

Visid regarded him unblinkingly, deciding within that it was safe to hate this man.

"There is . . . a special project for which you are being considered. I will recommend—continue to recommend—that you be turned down. You are too much a risk. If I am overruled, so be it. If you are accepted, so be it. If you are rejected from the program, either before or after, I will have your brain cleaned."

The teacher looked at his desk. "You may go."

The door out into the hallway slid open.

Visid sat unmoving, strange emotions churning within her.

The teacher looked up, blinking in surprise that she was still there.

"Well?" he said, his pale eyes on her.

"I hate you, too," she said, and ran out.

The attendant brought her to the usual transport departure tunnel and escorted her to a transport, empty save for herself, which brought her back to the dormitories. Outside the window, the afternoon still churned with blowing sand; the abated storm was returning with vigor. Far over the rim of Wells Crater, in the middle of the pit itself, a dust devil whipped itself mad, then ripped to nothingness. The lowering sun, pale orange and small, nothing at all like Venus's sun, looked frightened of the coming squall. It seemed to edge faster toward the horizon.

Venus.

Visid had not thought of it in a long time; indeed, there was little to think of. She remembered much of her father and more of her mother; she was present when her mother was killed during the Mars-Venus conflict. Or, as it was known on Mars, the One-Day War. Though—after her subsequent arrival, along with hundreds of other Venusian children, on Mars— much counseling had sought to eradicate the bad memories from her mind, the single image of her mother's body lying on the floor of her bedroom in two bisected parts was something that would never be stricken from her brain, even if the teacher had his way and had it wiped clean. Her father, she imagined, had been murdered by plasma soldiers the same way.

But she had been nine years old at the time, and little else in the way of Venusian memories remained. She did remember the sun as being larger and warmer, the sky as being pale blue instead of pink. The air on Venus smelled more like trees than Mars did, more of water than Mars. There was less dust. And she remembered the sight of a boat on a lake, and of a huge fish jumping from what looked like the sea. She thought her mother and father had taken her there but remembered nothing but these scattered images.

And yet after three years on Mars, she felt more of Venus than ever. Even if what she had in her mind was chimera, a false memory of a planet that was nothing like she imagined—indeed, the History lessons she had had on Venus showed images far more restrained and less romantic than those served up by her memory—those memories were more dear to her than vision of Mars. To her, Mars was, and would continue to remain, an alien planet.

And she felt no more than a visitor here.

The transport deposited her outside her dormitory building after the twenty-minute ride and immediately drove off. The dust storm was building to seriousness now. Shielding her eyes, Visid called for the dorm's entrance to extend its dust shield to her, but there was no response.

"Shield, extend!" she shouted above the whistle of wind; when there was still no activation, the momentary thrill of fear went through her that perhaps she had been deliberately locked out.

Those pale, steady eyes of the Culture teacher . . .

But then there was a grinding whir and the dorm's lobby shield, an opaque plastic, extended on its groaning hinges (the building was old) and engulfed her.

Instantly, the red dust, caught windless in the air, dropped around her, letting her breathe and see again.

"Whew!" she said.

To the tattoo of sand hitting the shield, she walked to the lobby door, which opened at her command, and entered the dorm.

The dorm attendant was in position in the lobby—but before it could quiz her, Visid said, in her own simulacrum of a robotic voice, "Visid Sneaden, entering."

"Very well," the attendant said, bowing stiffly from the waist; this one wore a tunic that hid all but its head, which shone like an ancient Earth toaster.

Hearing her own steps echo on the stone floor, she climbed the nearby stairwell to Level 2 and waited for that door to open for her.

At least there was some noise now.

She heard her own name in whispers, only magnified as she passed the first dormitory rooms on her right. Looking briefly in, she saw two students, Irma and Rainier Molton, sister and brother, staring back at her noncommittally. The dorm room's Screen was on, showing banks of arithmetic homework.

Returning their stares, she walked on.

Amie Carn, her roommate, was, at least, waiting for her in their room.

"Visid!" the younger girl cried, rising from her bed to fling her arms around her roommate. "We thought—"

"You thought what?" Visid said.

Amie removed her arms, was suddenly embarrassed. "Nothing. . . ."

"Thought they had wiped my brain? They will, but not yet. There's something happening."

Amie said, "There's talk of another war. It was on the Screen—"

"I knew it!" Visid cried. "Cornelian will go after Wrath-Pei now. But so far it's not going well."

"How do you know these things?" Amie looked genuinely surprised. "All they said—"

"—was what they want you to hear. You have to look between the words. The very fact that they tell us anything means it's serious, and that they'll want something from us."

Amie continued to pout. "And you shouldn't talk about the High Leader like that."

The older girl ignored her.

"And what did they keep you after lessons for?" Amie asked.

"Something about a special project. Maybe it will be my ticket out of here." She suddenly turned to her roommate. "But you're not to tell anyone about it, all right?"

"But what shall I say when they ask?"

"Tell them . . . anything you want. That they took preliminary measurements to clean my brain."

Amie's eyes widened. "Did they?"

"No. . . ."

But Visid Sneaden's thoughts were already elsewhere, connecting data into a scenario, fitting the snippets into a pattern, reading between words, cutting and pasting real fact and real culture and history and religion into a coherent picture that would give her the one thing in which she was interested, the one thing that would unlock so many puzzles about herself, this place where she was forced to be, and the place where she so desperately wanted to be—the one thing she would never stop looking for: the truth.

2

"This is not acceptable!"

Pynthas Rei already knew that, but was not about to say *anything* at the moment. To say anything might mean an end to his life—and, miserable as that life was at the moment, Pynthas wished to hang on to it for as long as possible.

The High Leader, formerly Prime Cornelian, towered over Pynthas like a huge metallic insect. His two sets of forward limbs, which served as hands, were strong enough to break a man in their grasp; Pynthas had seen the High Leader perform that particular trick on a few occasions. Reared up on his hind limbs, the High Leader doubled not only his height but his fearsomeness, and those forward limbs now hovered over Pynthas's trembling body, the sharp long fingers opening and closing like vises.

"Not acceptable!"

"Of course not, High Leader," Pynthas squeaked. Desperately, his eyes darted around his chamber for something to give the High Leader to crush—lest it be his own head. His eyes fixed on the nearest object, which he quickly grabbed and thrust up over his head.

The High Leader's nearest hand closed on it like a crab's claw—and it was only at this point that Pynthas's brain recorded the fact that he had just let the High Leader destroy one of his most precious personal objects—a ceramic figure in the shape of an Earth bear that his mother had given him when he was a boy.

A strangled whine began to form in his throat—but at the same moment he saw with relief that the High leader's mood had suddenly calmed and that he, Pynthas, would live through this day after all.

But still, his *bear* . . .

"Perhaps," the High Leader said, turning to pace the room, lowering the central limbs to make his gait resemble a bug with its front elevated, "there is something positive to be gained in this. It can be taken as a *good* sign. And, as always, it can be used to our advantage. You're sure this intelligence is reliable?"

Pynthas, ever the toady, instantly nodded his head in obeisance. "Absolutely, High Leader. The agents who perished getting us this information were all top-notch people."

"And how many of these outposts has Wrath-Pei taken?"

"Two, so far. On Oberon, Neried; there is indication that he means to attack Casto next."

"Let him have them."

Pynthas's mouth dropped open; he could not help his mouth from blurting, "What?"

The High Leader turned once more to face the

toady; but now there was a glint in his eye. "Yes, let Wrath-Pei have them all. If those outposts give him a heightened sense of security, he can possess them all."

"But, High Leader, if we try to get to Titan, it will be like going through a minefield to get to it!"

Annoyance clouded the High Leader's features, and Pynthas was instantly sorry he had spoken.

"Let me do your thinking for you, Pynthas," the High Leader snapped. "From now on I want you to be what you are: a part of the furniture in this room."

"Yes, High Leader!"

Pynthas stood very still, as if he were a lamp or ottoman; it took him a few moments to notice that the door had opened and slid closed and that the High Leader was gone.

Only then, when he was alone, did Pynthas Rei slump to the floor; his gaze fell on the shattered shards of his ceramic bear, and a tear came to his eye as he scooped them up; two of the larger pieces fit together into the chipped shape of the bear's happy grin.

"Oh, Mother!" Pynthas Rei sobbed, the shards dropping to the floor as Pynthas's briefly happy past came back to invade his thoughts.

Limb tips clicking on the steps like a dog's claws, the High Leader climbed, and arrived in no time at the garret room in which he kept Senator Kris. Chuckling at his own sobriquet for the chamber, the Museum, the High Leader entered, letting the door close behind him as his mechanical eyes adjusted to the gloom.

It was night outside in Lowell City; during the day the room's single cut of window presented a crawling oval of sunlight on the round walls; but tonight, with even the city's lights dulled by the growing dust storm, the room was barely illumined a dark orange, like pumpkin soup, with the senator's yellowish containment field in the center.

The High Leader wondered if the senator's weak eyes registered the color and brightness changes in the chamber; did he follow that bright oval around the wall during the daytime?

"Senator!" the High Leader said brightly. "How are you?"

Kris, suspended in an upright field that commenced a bare meter off the floor and held him in tight constraint, opened his weary eyes to gaze at the High Leader. For a few moments he said nothing; then the slightest of smiles crossed his lips.

"Cornelian," he said in a faraway whisper. "I take it you haven't found her yet."

The High Leader quashed the beginnings of peevishness. Instead, he said brightly, "No, I haven't, Senator! But I will!"

"How long has it been? Years?"

"Oh, yes, it's been three years, Kris. Two since our last visit together. And how are you faring?"

Kris tried to smile again, but instead winced. His body, a skeletal bag of bones, was so tightly held that any movement of face or limb caused discomfort.

The High Leader walked to the window and looked out. "When the dust isn't flying, it's truly a stunning view of Arsia Mons from here, if I remember correctly. Too bad you were put in the field facing the wall instead of the window, eh, Senator?" He turned and faced Kris again, who managed a smile at last.

The High Leader said, "You seem to have lost weight, Kris! Things aren't getting too roomy in there for you, are they?"

The High Leader moved to the containment control and snicked it the tiniest bit higher; the senator drew in his breath in pain.

"There, that's better, isn't it? Snug enough now?"

"You'll ... never . . . get what you . . . want from . . . her . . . Cornelian," Kris gasped.

"I'm sure I will, Kris. In fact, I wanted you to know that I'm about to move against Wrath-Pei. And when I do, my first order of business will be to return your daughter to Mars. And then—"

Despite the pain it caused him, Senator Kris grinned, gasping, "Never . . . Cornelian. . . ."

Suddenly angry, and afraid he might do more than he should to this man he still needed, the High Leader said "We'll see" and left the garret quickly, tweaking the containment control the tiniest bit tighter as he left, gaining at least a bit of satisfaction from the senator's moaning gasp.

3

Cold.

The world, for Dalin Shar, ruler of a world, was snow, and ice, and cold. He slept at night with the whistle of an icy wind in his ears, touched with the feel of frozen fingertips, listened with ears cold to the touch, watched with lidless eyes that stung from the tap of methane ice crystals. Warmth was something to dream about, something in another world of long ago. Warmth, and flowers, and sunlight, and the smell of roses, were something from a fairy tale told to a young boy—a young king in a mythical land that may have been called . . . Earth.

The fairy tale had a princess named Tabrel, who traveled to this mythical land and walked with the boy king in a garden. The air was scented with the perfume of velvety red roses, and the sky between the trellises was a brilliant shade of blue. There were fat white water clouds in the atmosphere. The afternoon brushed their skins with the heavenly warmth of a nearby star.

And then the young man, thinking to be fey, suddenly stopped and looked into the princess' eyes—

and was locked there forever. And what began as a stolen kiss and flirtation became something that would never end, a moment captured forever in time, when the boy king and the princess felt their hearts suddenly open and flow together, mingling, becoming one. . . .

Lidless under an ocher moon, Dalin Shar, who was ruler of faraway Earth, thought of his first true-love kiss.

He could see Tabrel in his mind's eye. Standing on this frozen bluff, with half of Pluto spread out far and wide beneath him like a cracked translucent blue plate; with the dropping, deadly cold penetrating the ripped rags of his thermal suit, and pellets of frozen methane hard as tiny stones pelting his cheeks; with the plum-colored glow of the descended SunOne at the horizon, its waning heat and light still washing the moon Charon with deep lemon; here, in this frigid hell, Dalin closed his mind's eye and felt not the cold, not the sting of methane crystals, but the incredibly warm softness of the first touch of Tabrel's lips on his own as he stood with her in his own fragrant gardens, on an Earth that was surely not mythical yet seemed a lifetime away. . . .

"Dalin! It's time to come in before you freeze, boy! Hurry up now!"

Dalin felt an insistent pull at his elbow.

The warm Earthly gardens, the kiss, all of it dissolved, leaving Dalin Shar's lidless open eyes with the pale, hateful, rutted view of Pluto's moon. Charon had shifted in its orbit toward the horizon, following the dimming purple glow of SunOne. Soon

SunOne, in its own orbit slightly faster than Charon, would pull its miserly light away, and the moon would revert to its dull, dead, nearly unseen norm in the sky. It was, after all, a lump of ice and rock not much different from a comet.

A dirty snowball.

"Dalin!" the voice close by his ear rasped again. The pull on Dalin's sleeve became more insistent. "Use your head, Sire! Come in now!"

Dalin turned his face into the nearly constant eight-mile-per-hour wind of Pluto's surface. The atmosphere was so tenuous, held by Pluto's weak gravity and fed by the warming effects of SunOne, that it had at first been thought that no winds at all might form.

But weather was something nearly as voracious as life, and there were even thin clouds of water that occasionally rose like wraiths, when the planet's surface was turned toward the distant starlike Sun, which nevertheless added its own bulblike solar energy to SunOne—enough, at least, to form the ghost clouds that swept constantly like a broom to the dirty surface of the dirty planet.

It was in these seasons when the wind rose above the maddening eight-mile-per-hour level to sometimes roar in storms that covered the planet in a dirty blue blanket of ice and snow.

"Dalin!" Shatz Abel's voice rasped. His grip was like that of an iron vise.

"All right," Dalin said somberly.

For a moment he looked into Shatz Abel's bearded visage.

"Follow me!" the pirate said urgently.

Dalin nodded.

He bowed into the wind, following Shatz Abel in line like one of two monks. But these clerics were not praying; they were guarding their faces from cutting crystals of methane, which could wear away features given enough time, even as they constantly reshaped the ugly cold blue face of Pluto.

They trudged the path they both knew so well back to shelter. The wind was a constant whine, like torture, in their ears, and now Dalin felt where the ice crystals had burned against his unprotected face.

They bowed under the eaves of their cave and entered their shelter, which was tunneled into the side of an icy hill.

Shatz Abel immediately closed the stainless door to seal the structure.

"Quickly!" he said, throwing back Dalin's hood. "Let me see what you've done to yourself!"

The light, though purposefully dim in the shelter, hurt Dalin's eyes. He sat tiredly on the chair that Shatz Abel thrust beneath him, and subjected himself to the man's probings of his face and hands.

"I told you to discard these gloves a week ago!" Shatz Abel scolded. He dropped Dalin's reddened hands and shambled off to one end of the shelter, rattling through an old medicine cabinet. His gait was like a bear's.

"You're a fool!" Shatz Abel said, shuffling back with one of his inevitable tubes of ointment, which he began to smear sloppily across Dalin's knuckles. Vaguely, there was pain that Dalin chose to ignore.

Shatz Abel paused in his slathering to look up angrily at the younger man. "You'll murder yourself yet!"

"I don't care if I die."

Shatz Abel's angered continued. "Don't care? Don't you care about the people carrying on your fight for you?"

Dalin looked at him blankly. "As far as I'm concerned, they don't exist."

Shatz Abel raised an ointment-stained hand and brought it sharply across the young man's face.

"How *dare* you!" he shouted.

Anger flared through Dalin. Snapping out of his reverie, he brought his own hand up and held it above Shatz Abel, balling it into a fist.

The two men looked at one another, and suddenly the pirate laughed.

"Look at you!" the pirate said. "Three years on this rock, and in some ways you're still the boy you were when you arrived here! True, you're inches taller, and a bit broader in the chest; and, someday soon, you may even have to shave your whiskers—" with a chuckle, the pirate tried to brush his hand across Dalin's still mostly smooth chin; the king knocked Shatz Abel's fingers away with a sour look, "but in some ways, you still act like a child! True, you can pull your weight when work needs to be done, arm wrestle well enough to at least give me a challenge— and you *did* save my skin last year when you deflected our falling antenna mast from my skull. And true: you have lost a bit of your courtly impudence, and deprivation has curbed your selfish instincts.

And yet, in certain areas . . ." The pirate left off, still grinning.

Dalin stared at him, anger held.

"Go ahead, boy—hit me, if it makes you feel better."

Suddenly all anger drained from Dalin, and he dropped his hand to his lap again. "It's just that none of it matters to me if . . ."

Shatz Abel stood up and laughed. "The young man in love!"

Now Dalin's anger flared again and held, as he launched himself at the burly pirate, who was shuffling back to his medicine cabinet to replace the salve.

Dalin struck Shatz Abel, knocking him down, then stood over the older man as Shatz Abel turned himself over, looking up at Dalin and bringing a hand across his cut lip.

"The young man in love . . ."

"Yes! I love her!"

"Even though you know nothing of her for three long years—" Shatz Abel began.

The two men were distracted by a scratching at the metal door, which rose to a constant tapping hiss.

"The wind is picking up," Shatz Abel said. His brow furrowed as he pushed himself to his feet, dabbing a final time at the blood on the corner of his lip. "This storm will be worse than the last."

Dalin was staring at the door. "The last storm lasted a month."

Shatz Abel humphed. "In any event, we'd better cover the dish and stow the outside gear."

Dalin nodded.

Shatz Abel regarded him. "Are you all right now, boy?"

"No," Dalin said. But the color had returned to his cheeks, and there was life in his eyes.

Shatz Abel gave a short laugh and slapped the young man's back as he passed him on the way to the heavy clothing lockers near the outer door. "We'll make a king of you yet. At least you're alive. And while you're alive, there's hope." He paused. "For everything."

Dalin nodded, and before long the two men were shrugging into heavy clothing, with masks for protection and heavy, servo-driven gloves.

Shatz Abel, straining, opened the stainless steel door with a curse.

As Dalin came up beside him, the pirate took the boy by the scruff of his neck and pointed north, at a dim greenish patch of light between two tall mountains whose tops were already shrouded in lowering storm clouds.

"There it is," Shatz Abel said. "Tombaugh City. Our Holy Grail, and ticket off Pluto. And now that Wrath-Pei has finally turned his attention away from us, that's what we head for. I've waited nine years and you've waited three for this trip, but it will probably kill us both. A hundred kilometers distant, and not one of them easy. If the panthers don't get us, the white bears will try; and if they both lose out, the weather will take their place. I've never been crazy enough to go myself, and not only because there's a price on my head there. It's a trip for madmen and fools. We must be both, because now we're

going to make that trip, boy, you and me, and then
the two of us are going to have one good meal under
SunOne, and then buy or steal our way off Pluto."

"You're . . . hurting me," Dalin croaked.

Still holding Dalin tightly, as a child might hold a
kitten by the scruff of the neck, Shatz Abel turned
the king's face so that the boy's lidless eyes were
staring into his own bloodshot ones.

"And nothing's going to stop us from getting off
Pluto and back to Earth. Nothing. And if you want
that girl of yours to be your queen, you'd better start
believing what I say."

He released Dalin, and the king stumbled and fell
to the ground.

"Now come with me, Sire, and do what has to
be done."

Shatz Abel closed the door to their shelter behind
them and headed off into the howl of ice and wind.

Dalin rose and followed; and out in the growing
storm, doing what had to be done, Dalin once again
thought of that first kiss. . . .

4

Wrath-Pei was . . . happy.

Which disturbed him greatly. It was not that he was adverse to pleasure—in fact, he had devoted his life to it. And though many of his pleasures were what other men deemed perversions . . . well, this did not bother him greatly. He was proud of his sociopathology; truly, he reveled in it. *If a man is fully what he is*, so his philosophy went, *then what's the problem?* How could you fault a man for being himself? And Wrath-Pei had always been so much . . . *himself*.

But happiness, which Wrath-Pei equated with ease of acquisition, bothered him to the core. Made him almost frown. He was used to getting what he wanted—had gotten what he wanted since taking his first toy from his only sibling at the age of one and discovering that the act gave him pleasure, all the more enhanced by the subsequent destruction of that toy. Oh, the tears and rage that act had produced! How his sibling had wailed with despair!

And what a wondrous rush of warm pleasure had

flowed through Wrath-Pei's body, even tingling his skin!

But had the actual taking of that toy been an easy event? Of course not! There had been fighting, and one-year-old words of recrimination, fear, and hatred, and a tug-of-war—but finally the prize had been gained and the fluid flow of pure satisfaction attained at the outcome.

And the fight itself had been part of the pleasure!

But now . . . things were going too easily. Wrath-Pei had expected some sort of obstacle to be thrown in his path by now—but none had come. It was almost as if the *Bug*, Prime Cornelian—or, as he fancied himself, High Leader—could not be bothered. As if Wrath-Pei didn't matter enough to be stopped at the moment. And though Wrath-Pei knew this wasn't true in essence—he knew Cornelian much too well, knew that the *Bug* seethed at each Outer Planets outpost that Wrath-Pei plucked like a cherry from the High Leader's tree—still Wrath-Pei was made uneasy by the ease with which these cherries were falling into his hand.

There were, of course, reasons: Cornelian had his hands full with other matters at the moment, including, prominently, the growing trouble on Earth—but, even so, couldn't the High Leader devote even a *tiny* bit of his attention and boundless rage to his old enemy Wrath-Pei?

Just to make things . . . spicier?

Oh, well, Wrath-Pei thought, *we'll just have to make our fun without him for the moment.*

The time would come, soon enough.

Oh, yes, it would.

Smiling in his thoughts, floating in his gyro-controlled chair, which enfolded his sitting body like a hand holding one of those cherries, Wrath-Pei did not notice the soothing beep of a message-waiting summons on the glowing Screen before him. There came the gentlest of taps on his black-leather-clad shoulder, and Wrath-Pei turned to see Lawrence, just lowering the stump of his left arm; behind his visor, which covered nearly all of his face save his thin lips, the lower of which had been clipped neatly away, showing the young man's gum line and a row of perfect teeth, Lawrence's expression was unreadable.

"Message, Your Eminence," the boy said.

Gently shaken from his reverie, Wrath-Pei turned to the Screen and arched a silver eyebrow.

"Perhaps something . . . interesting?" he said, and ordered the Screen to proceed with the message, even as Lawrence stepped back away from the chair, his lidless eyes no doubt already returning to their task of studying the lines of data that continuously flowed across his visor.

On the Screen, Wrath-Pei was presented with the always-unsmiling visage of Kamath Clan, of Titan.

"My queen!" Wrath-Pei said in delight. "What a pleasure to see you!"

"A pleasure I cannot reciprocate." Kamath Clan said dourly.

"What a shame!"

"Shame has everything to do with my call," Kamath Clan said.

"Then by all means elaborate!" Wrath-Pei said, the pleasure of the queen's displeasure already beginning to give his skin the familiar tingle he had so missed lately.

Barely contained rage filled the queen's features, no doubt fueled by Wrath-Pei's delighted visage.

"*Quog!*" she burst out, her face reddening.

"What of him? He is well, I hope?"

"He has vanished!"

Wrath-Pei let a fraction of his smile dip into pity. "How . . . terrible!"

"What have you done with him?" the queen demanded. "I still have my sources, and they tell me you have spirited him away to your *ship*! Return him immediately!"

All of Wrath-Pei's smile returned. "Now, my queen, please don't be so upset. After all, I've just managed a great coup for you and your sect. From now on, the sulfur fields on Io, sacred as they are to you, will be provided duty-free to all of Titan! Isn't that marvelous? No more tribute to the Martians, no more cash on the barrelhead for your most revered of ceremonial substances. I should think all Titanians—and most especially yourself—would be singing my praises in the Temple of Faran Clan. Why, I've just made religion . . . cheaper!"

"I repeat: what have you done with Quog!"

"Quog is . . . safe. And will continue to be safe. The truth is, the man never got out, and I thought it was time he enjoyed a vacation. In payment for all the . . . service he has rendered to you over the years.

In fact, you could say I did it all for you, my queen! And when he returns, he'll be rested and happy—and of even more service than ever!"

"Bring him back immediately!"

"That isn't . . . feasible, my queen. There are some . . . experiments that we are conducting, Quog and I, that are in a delicate stage at the moment. But you'll see him again soon enough."

Wrath-Pei was nearly swimming in the delicious sensations that Kamath Clan's face presented him: rage, sickness, and, yes, terror!

The queen's face collapsed with the weight of that last manifestation, and suddenly, if Wrath-Pei was capable of feeling pity, he would have felt it.

"Please bring him back," Kamath Clan begged.

"Soon . . . enough."

The queen's voice became hoarse, all pretense of royalty gone. "I implore you."

"What would you say, my queen, if I told you that there is a possibility of . . . duplication of Quog's gifts. He is old, you know, and not likely to live forever."

"I've tried, myself. It is useless!"

"Perhaps not. Do you think I . . . borrowed Quog merely to . . . deny you?"

The flaring of bright hope on her face was not nearly as satisfying as her former terror.

Wrath-Pei waited a moment, and then asked sweetly, "And how is your son, Jamal? Is he . . . well?"

Rage returned. "You cannot have him!"

"Nevertheless—"

The Screen went blank.

Wrath-Pei stared at the vacant Screen for a moment, remembering each instant he had just experienced as if savoring it for the first time. Had he been the one to cut the transmission? Had Lawrence done it for him? Or had Kamath Clan?

No matter; the timing had been exquisite.

The look on her face . . .

Wrath-Pei closed his eyes for a moment, drinking the last drop of Kamath Clan's despair.

Then, summoning Lawrence to him he thought it was time to fill his eyes with another, allied sight that might give him . . . pleasure.

The ship was cavernous, but with Lawrence's guidance of the gyro chair they had reached the appointed deck and cabin in no time.

The door slid open at Wrath-Pei's arrival.

At Quog's own request, the room was kept dark. Not wanting to upset the old man more than was necessary, Wrath-Pei had had as near a duplicate of Quog's quarters as possible constructed. With a little imagination, the inside of Deck 5, Cabin 14 looked very much like the old man's cave of a hovel in the Ruz Balib section of his home on Titan. Care had been taken even to cover the various potion bottles on the shelves with the proper amount of dust.

From the corner of the room, in shadows out of even the weak light that suffused the gloom, Quog's weak voice said, "Wrath-Pei . . ."

"Yes!" Wrath-Pei said brightly, moving deeper into

the cabin; in the darkest corner he could just make out the outline of the old man's figure now.

"How . . . goes it, Wrath-Pei?" Quog said in a dreamy whisper. He chuckled, a dry rasp. "Do you think you will succeed where Kamath Clan, and others, have failed?"

"I certainly intend to," Wrath-Pei said. "And even if I do not, a . . . synthesis of what you have to offer is only secondary to my needs, anyway."

"I thought as much. Though I am not a political man myself."

"All men are politicians."

Quog laughed his crackly rasp. "How true. May I ask you a question, Wrath-Pei?"

"I am in a generous mood."

"Good. I admire generosity, since I have been so generous with my existence myself. My question is: have you ever thought of . . . *sampling*, yourself?"

"Me?" Wrath-Pei was nearly startled—and that fact startled him. "Of course not."

"As all men are politicians, but all men also seek to . . . remember."

"I have all the memories I need, Quog, and I keep them in their place."

"Do you? Wouldn't you like to . . . *see* again, with the same vision you had? To *experience* what you have possessed, as if you were possessing it for the first time?"

For once direct, Wrath-Pei said, "It never occurred to me."

Quog's chuckle was broken in half by a weak cough. "You seem a prime candidate to me."

"Perhaps. But to tell you the truth, I have just as much fun with my present memories as my past ones." He thought briefly of Kamath Clan's face. "And to be even more truthful, the thought of . . . *using* is abhorrent to me."

"It was just a question, Wrath-Pei."

"Yes, I'm sure it was."

To Lawrence, Wrath-Pei said, "Closer."

Lawrence edged the gyro chair closer to the old man. The shadows retreated slightly, giving form to outline. Quog's body, self-trussed, suspended upside down, still could not in any way be called human. Its sideways bend, courtesy of the Puppet Death he had endured at the age of eighteen, culminated in tiny deformed feet that barely afforded him a shuffling gait; at the other extreme, his taffylike, limb-thin face resembled layers of melted plastic. In the midst of this visage his organs of sight, odor, and hearing were compressed to little more than slits. His mouth was an oval, vertical hole.

From portions of Quog's naked body, his disfigured, three-fingered hands, his chest, his thighs, his neck, dripped a thickly viscous substance, dark brown in color, which slowly collected in a pan beneath the old man's head. Its dripping made a sound like oil into a pool.

"As you said, Quog," Wrath-Pei said, fully enjoying the sight of the old man's body, a disfigurement of the human form that left Wrath-Pei in awe of Nature, his only rival, "all men are politicians. What is your affiliation?"

"Me?" Quog said dreamily, weakly, from deep

within his own memories. "Why, if pressed to admit it, Wrath-Pei"—and now his voice broke into a rasping, coughing laugh—"I would have to say I belong to anywhere but now."

5

For Co-Prime Minister Besh, things had gone from bad to worse.

Through the window of his office, spring was turning to summer. It would be warm and dry, according to the forecasts; already a drought was under way in the western provinces, and the governor of India was fairly begging for wheat.

That which was not to be had.

Too bad Labor Minister Rere had chosen to stand with the King, Dalin Shar, three years ago; they could have used his expertise now.

This was not the way Besh had imagined hegemony. Even as a young boy, watching the struggles during Sarat Shar's long consolidation of power, he knew that the intricacies, the Machiavellian subtleties, of rule were something that he wanted to devote his life to. Always an avid chess player, he still kept the same two books at his bedside that had been there since he was thirteen: *The Prince*, and Argmon-Fei's *Chess: The Eternal Struggle*. And still, every night before retiring, he read a chapter from each, though he long since had memorized both.

In his pride, he had thought that such traits as these would one day make his biography (or autobiography, since he also fancied himself a writer and had also, since the age of thirteen, kept a meticulous diary) required reading for all citizens of Earth; perhaps, even, all the Worlds.

Now he knew that he should have spent less of his time playing chess and learning tactics, and more time learning how to use a dagger.

What had begun as an enterprise of (in Co-Prime Minister Besh's mind, at least) patriotrism had lately turned into a nightmare.

Co-Prime Minister Acron, of course, was the problem.

But what a problem! How best to rid oneself of a street thug? None of the subtle ways had worked. On half a dozen occasions in the last thirty-six months Besh had tried to legally oust Acron from his position; on each occasion, the stout bully had remained, at the end of the maneuver, exactly where he had been to begin with. He was like some horrible toy, an air-filled, bobbing thing that, when pressed underwater, comes right back to the surface, smiling and bobbing once more.

Even the High Leader, whose efforts on Besh's behalf had, admittedly, been tepid, had been unable to shift the balance of power Besh's way. But then, that was Cornelian's style, to divide and dominate. It had been the High Leader's will to let Acron rule alongside Besh, had it not? Not that it had done much good in the long run, with the entirety of Earth now on the brink of outright rebellion and the fragile alliances and subtle balances Besh had spent the last half decade forming crumbling around them all.

Oh! The plans Besh had had in his head for Earth! The delicate levers he had yearned to pull, ever since those teenage years of dreaming! He had known since then that he had greatness in him—and had planned, since then, to let that greatness flower. All those years watching Prime Minister Faulkner's clumsy rule, as proxy to the brat Dalin Shar—how Besh had longed to take the reins then! But no, he had waited and schemed, putting off his plans, whiling his hours with ones and zeroes as finance minister. . . .

And now that he sat in the seat he had so long coveted, it all seemed so . . . empty.

Outside Besh's window, waves of heat were already building. He could just make out the top of the trellises in what had once been the Imperial rose gardens; the petalless vines were dry and brittle, a crown of thorns. There hadn't been roses for three years, and even then they had made it on their own, without watering. That summer had been wetter than most.

There came a light knock—almost reverential—on the door to Besh's office.

"Come in," Besh said.

The door opened, revealing a guard in dun-colored uniform and shaved head beneath his cap; he was young and nervous.

"It's time, Co-Prime Minister."

"Is it?" Time had passed quickly during his ruminations; it must already be nearing noon.

"Very well," Besh said, rising.

Outside the window, between the Imperial Palace and the dried twigs of the rose gardens, stood a flat of ground cleared of all obstacles; at one end a wall of neatly stacked sandbags stood, before which was a single chair. Thirty paces away stood ten riflemen, checking their rasers.

Turning away from the window, Besh smiled tiredly at the young guard in the doorway.

"Don't worry, son," he said, "I won't run away on you."

"No, sir," the guard said, eyes downward.

Besh left his office and was surprised to see Co-Prime Minister Acron, florid-faced, waiting for him in the hallway.

"I would have thought you'd be gloating in your chambers," Besh said.

Acron approached him quickly, drawing a short-handled blade from his tunic with resolve. He took Besh's arm in a tight grip while thrusing the dagger in below the breastbone and driving upward. Acron's eyes never left Besh's face.

"*I wanted to do this myself,*" he hissed.

After shocked surprise, Besh's face began to collapse, but he managed to keep his gaze focused on Acron for a moment.

"I'm not . . . surprised . . ."

Acron let him go, and Besh collapsed to the ground, drawing a last breath before lying still.

Acron turned angrily to the wide-eyed young guard.

"Get rid of him, *now*," Acron said. "And say nothing, or you'll follow his example."

Without another word, Co-Prime Minister Acron turned on his heel and marched off to a prior engagement.

"You are here because the time for finesse is over," Acron said. Standing with the flats of his hands on the table before him, he leveled a hard look at the four men seated around the table; three were already his own, and the fourth was needed. "Besh is gone, and I am as of this moment assuming the full prime minister's mantle, with concurrent powers."

"It was a shame about poor Besh," Law Minister Chang said with barely suppressed glee. "My court had no choice but to find him guilty of sedition, of course."

"He never made it to the firing squad," Acron said, and watched Chang's smile falter. Chang was a good bureaucrat, but, like the late Besh, was too subtle for his own good. "I dispatched him myself. Are there any objections?"

Acron was pleased at the looks on their faces; and pleased that you could have heard a pin drop in the room.

"Now that Besh is gone, our real work begins. *With or without the High Leader's help.*"

This was the big step; for a moment he thought there would be no objection, but then the one question mark of the group, Cornelian's diplomat and spy Cal-Fen, spoke up.

"Is that wise, Co-Prime—pardon me, *Prime* Minister? You are aware that the High Leader approved of your recent . . . realignment of power. The High Leader has every confidence in your abilities, and knows that the current troubles with the outer provinces will be resolved, as well as the disturbances in the cities. As the High Leader's representative, I can assure you that relations between Earth and Mars have never been better than they are at this moment. And we see nothing but a continuance of the current special status, shall we say, of the relations of our two worlds—"

Barely taking a breath, Acron cut the man off. "Mars and Earth will continue to be friends, Ambassador Cal-Fen, as long as Mars does not meddle in Earth's affairs. Let us call this a new era of cooperation."

Cal-Fen gave a diplomat's smile and prepared to launch into another flowery speech, which Acron snuffed before it could begin.

"A new era," the prime minister said coldly, "in which Earth takes care of its own problems."

For emphasis, Acron drew the knife he had so recently slipped between Besh's ribs and threw it on the table, where it came to rest pointing at the Martian ambassador. Its reddened tip was like an accusing finger.

"Let me be blunt, Ambassador," Acron said. "I am going to crush the rebellion on Earth, and, in the process, I am going to crush any Earthling with sympathetic ties to Mars. As of this moment Earth and Mars are once again two separate worlds. And you will be on a shuttle home to Mars tonight, to deliver that message personally to the High Leader."

Ambassador Cal-Fen rose; for a moment he sought to lock stares with Acron, but when the prime minister reached over to retrieve his dagger, bringing it up under the ambassador's chin and nicking it with the blade before sheathing it, Cal-Fen's eyes widened and he gave up, turned on his heel, and marched out of the room.

When the door had slid closed behind him, Acron laughed, but his laughter was the only sound in the room.

"Relax, gentlemen," Acron said, sitting down and taking a hugely deep breath. "I have no intention of breaking ties with Mars. That little charade was for Ambassador Cal-Fen's benefit. The High Leader asked me to send him home with his tail between his legs; it seems he's been skimming profit money from some of the Martian textile concerns here, and not sharing the proceeds. I'm afraid he has a fate similar to Besh's waiting for him when he gets home."

Prime Minister Acron's florid face broke into a grin; and in a moment the other ministers, led by Chang, were guffawing at the joke.

"And now," Acron said, "we really do have much work to do."

And in the back of Prime Minister Acron's iron mind was the thought, *No intention of breaking ties with Mars—yet.*

6

The summons came at the oddest time: in the middle of the night.

Visid awoke, feeling a nearby presence. The room was etched in shadows; Amie was soundly asleep on her opposite pallet, head turned outward, mouth slightly open, breathing like a child; from out in the hallway came the softly unending murmur of Lessons, the osmotic drone of hidden voices telling Venusian children, even in the midst of dreams, that they were destined to serve their home planet and destined to serve their Martian masters.

And yet—

Visid looked at the doorway; something was blocking it.

An attendant: a box on wheels, a primitive retriever model.

"You will come with me," the attendant said.

Visid rose.

"Dress." the attendant said. "Quietly."

Visid did as she was told.

In a few moments she was leaving the room, looking back at Amie, still asleep. One of her friend's hands trailed over the side of the pallet, fingertips touching the floor.

"Good-bye," Visid whispered, and followed the attendant into the hallway and out to a waiting transport.

For the second time in a month, she had a transport to herself.

But now it was nighttime, and the stars were out. She knew the Martian names for constellations from Lessons: Great Pot, Small Pot, Hourglass. Once, there had been a lesson under the stars, on a dusty night, with an ancient telescope. None of what she had seen had been as vivid as Screen images; dust had finally covered the instrument's lens with a thin coat, and they had gone back into the dormitory.

But the stars tonight were beautiful, and there were many more than she had imagined. As so often happened, when the dust storm ended a week ago it had drawn any moisture in the air with it; and when the winds had died, all the muck of the atmosphere had dropped to Mars' surface in a cleansing dry rain that left the sky clean, clear, cold.

There was Earth, a tiny blue smudge, over the horizon, with its white moon a nearby dot; and higher up what must be Jupiter, huge, a gibbous lantern whose bands of color she could almost see without optical aid.

She wished she had that telescope now!

And there—

Venus.

It was unmistakable, well below Jupiter and to

Earth's right, near the horizon. It was not large, but was nevertheless softly brilliant, unmistakably a planet. Visid had read that before the terraforming of Venus had begun it had been twice as bright, due to the constant cloud cover and the planet's nearness to the Sun. In Screen images, the old Venus had looked yellow-white; now its color was more muted, a golden red with growing patches of blue-green.

Beautiful.

Home.

Someday . . .

She watched for what seemed like hours, until the rusty rose of dawn began to creep over the east.

Visid's waking dream was broken by the transport stopping before the school's administration building; out front, barely illumined in coming morning light, was a lone, tall figure.

Oh, no . . .

The transport stopped; but to Visid's surprise she was not told to depart; instead, the figure, which was that of the teacher of Culture, rail-thin and tall, stooped to step up onto the bus.

The teacher's eyes regarded her with a strange look; a mixture of disapproval and extreme curiosity—as if she were a bad new bug under a Biology microviewer.

"The doors in these transports are not tall enough," he said in preamble, then added: "For some reason, you have been chosen for the project we spoke of three weeks ago."

Visid's heart leaped with excitement, but she kept

her face stoic in reaction to the teacher's continued scowl.

"I used my position here as chancellor—yes, child, I am more than just an instructor—to try to prevent this decision's implementation, but to no avail." His scowl deepened. "However, I was given assurance that if you don't work out, you will be returned here and I may institute the brain cleaning I so forcefully insisted that you require."

Sensing that no matter what happened in the future, she would be free of this man, Visid allowed a smile to cross swords with the chancellor's frown.

"You may not smile for long," the chancellor said, turning to duck under the transport's door. In a moment, as the door slid shut, he stood in his former position, sourly watching the transport pull away as red dawn rose.

As her window passed his position, Visid said "I will always hate you!" and was pleased to see his reaction of anger.

"That's one bridge burned," she said to herself; but found an odd comfort in the thought, as the transport pulled away, leaving the school and the chancellor behind as only memories, shrinking in view.

An hour later found her within the outskirts of Lowell City, as dawn turned into a workday, with the concurrent crowding of streets.

Visid had never been in traffic before. On her infrequent trips into the city, she and the other students had always been well chaperoned by attendants. The trips had been point-to-point affairs; they had traveled in darkness to a museum or off-school teaching facility, had spent the day in said facility performing specific learning tasks, and then had traveled back to their dormitory in darkness. Lowell had never been seen alive.

But today, in bright morning light, the city fairly burst with energy. Transports hemmed them in on either side; their forward progress was impeded by a long line of vehicles in front of them. The sandstone-paved streets were wide, but seemingly not wide enough; there didn't seem to be enough room for everyone, walkers and riders.

"Attendant," Visid queried the transport driver, "is it always this crowded?"

"Only at this time, and in the evening, when workers depart for their homes," the robot answered. It added, "You must remember that there are nearly three times as many pedestrians in the underground walkways and transport tunnels at this moment."

"Wow. And where do they all work?"

"There was a moment a hesitation, which led Visid to believe she had asked a silly question.

"There are approximately sixteen thousand, four hundred different occupations in Lowell City, beginning with the most densely filled position, Martian defense worker, followed by Martian Marine, followed by—"

"Thank you, Attendant. That will be enough."

"As you wish."

"Tell me, though: when will we arrive at our destination?"

"Traffic permitting, within five minutes."

Just then there was a break in the transport line in front of them, and their own vehicle shot ahead, making an abrupt right turn that brought it onto the straightaway bordering the Great Lawn, which led directly, blocks ahead, to the former residence of the High Perfect of Mars; its pink sandstone form was unmistakable, grand as it was, narrowing as it did to a single garret topped with a sickle within a circle of black iron, the symbol of Martian solidarity (and, lately, aggression) that scraped the pink sky.

Visid felt herself go cold inside.

"Attendant," she asked, "where are we going?"

Without turned from his driving, the attendant said, "Rear entrance bay number four."

"Of the residence of the High Prefect?"

"High *Leader*. Correct."

"Am I to meet with the High Leader?" Visid asked; she recalled the chancellor's last words to her: *You may not smile for long.*

"That I do not know."

To their left, the empty expanse of the Great Lawn gave way abruptly to the shadowing, looming bulk of the residence; the temperature seemed to drop within the transport.

"Attendant," Visid said, "let me out here."

"We are not yet at our destination."

With sudden foreboding, Visid rose from her seat as the transport began to descend an incline and pink stone walls rose up on either side of them. Unsteadily, she walked to the front of the transport, descended into the exit well, and tried to pry open the door.

The attendant turned his chromed head in her direction.

"We will be stopping soon," he said. "Please return to your seat."

"Let me out now!"

"That is not allowable."

"Let me out!"

The attendant turned its attention back to driving, while its right hand let go of the transport's drive bar and reached out to restrain Visid in a tight grasp.

"Let me go!"

"I am not allowed to harm you, but I must keep you in this position until we reach our destination."

They were nearly in darkness as the transport continued down the incline; now dim lights showed them a docking bay area as the transport's angle evened out.

"We are nearly there," the attendant said.

There was a single dark opening ahead of them, labeled overhead with the number 4; a single figure stood regarding the slowing transport.

For a moment Visid's heart skipped; the figure was tall and angularly thin, and she was struck with the flashing certainty that a cruel joke had been played on her: that the chancellor had somehow raced ahead of her to this spot, where he waited to drag her to the brain cleaning he so desperately wanted her to undergo.

"*Oh, no . . .*" Visid said.

The transport stopped and stood idling with a pleasant hum while the figure in the doorway slowly approached.

The attendant continued to hold Visid in an iron grip as the figure outside, its face still hidden in the entrance bay's gloom, now stood before the transport's door. Visid, trapped in the exit bay, was a mere arm's length away from the man, who now made an impatient motion for the transport's door to open.

The attendant activated the door, which slid open; at the same time, the attendant let Visid go.

Off balance, she fell out of the transport's exit well, into the arms of the startled figure outside, who clumsily caught her.

Even in the gloom, she could now make out the features of the figure supporting her.

It was not the chancellor.

She gasped anyway, stifling a scream at the horrible visage she beheld: a grossly high forehead leading to a balding pate of lank, long yellow-gray hair; the skin was sallow and pale, deeply pocked about the eyes and sunken cheeks. The eyes were set in hollows and were a brackish color, the whites bleeding sickly into the irises. The mouth's lips were missing, presenting a mouth full of bad teeth in a perpetual, rictuslike smile.

"I am," the figure said, "Sam-Sei, the Machine Master of Mars."

Now Visid, unable to scream, fainted instead.

"And you," the Machine Master concluded, "are here to assist me."

7

"Dig, damn you!"

"I *am* digging!"

For the thirtieth time that day, Dalin wanted to turn his shovel from the job at hand to the back of Shatz Abel's head. The burly pirate was a madman, and everyone knew that the only way to stop a madman was by any means possible.

The flat side of a shovel, for instance.

Above the howl of wind, Dalin heard Shatz Abel's laughter close by. He turned, and the few, minuscule, unprotected portions of his face—between visor and face mask, between hood and neck—stung with the pelt of tiny, unending methane crystals. How he hated this snow! How he hated the fact that it sang when it fell, the crystals scraping one against the other in an unearthly high, pinging hiss. And how he hated, most of all, the fact that it wouldn't stop!

Shatz Abel's face, a few feet away, broke into a smile around his mouth hole. Again the pirate laughed.

"Tired, are we, Your Majesty? Perhaps a cup of tea on the veranda, overlooking the gardens? Perhaps a hot bath, drawn by your valet? Perhaps a warm kiss in a rose garden—"

"Shut your mouth!"

Shatz Abel laughed the louder. Though by now Dalin knew that the bearded freebooter goaded him for his own good, as he had been doing for the last three years, it did not make it any easier to take.

In frustration and mostly anger, the King turned from Shatz Abel, thrust his shovel into the thickening pile of blue-white snow mounting around the storage shed, and began to dig again.

"Ha!" Shatz Abel said.

Suddenly Dalin threw down his shovel and faced the man again.

"When will it end?" he shouted, anger giving way to frustration now.

The pirate laughed. "Perhaps never! Maybe they'll find us a hundred years from now, my liege, just as we are today! Frozen in place with our shovels— perhaps you'll freeze solid as you stand over me, ready to strike me with your oversized spoon!"

Shatz Abel began to laugh hysterically—and now Dalin had the frightening thought that perhaps this huge man, who, even though he was boorish, vexatious, and loud, the king had come to depend on, had lost his own mind after so many years on Pluto. Nine years must be an eternity to a man such as Shatz Abel: and now, perhaps this last storm, already by the pirate's admission exceeding in length and ferocity anything he had ever seen on the planet, had done him in. Nearly six weeks it had been storming, the wind at a constant howl, the snow falling at an incessant rate, requiring them to order their days by the storm's clock, and each day uncover their supply shed and equipment tower lest they disappear from sight forever. Each day they ate the same food, drank the same store of tea, repeated the same conversations, and harbored the same thoughts. Each day had become like the last, which had been like the one before.

"Ha ha!" Shatz Abel whooped, throwing his shovel into the air where it disappeared into a blowing cloud of snow and was lost.

"What are you doing!" Dalin said in alarm; he approached the pirate, who was now jumping into the air, letting his huge body land in the most convenient drift of snow underneath.

"Ha!" Shatz Abel shouted.

Now Dalin Shar stood over the other man, gripping his shovel like the weapon he had fantasized about.

The pirate looked up at him and produced fresh laughter.

"Ha! Young King Shar, you now present the picture I proposed! Go ahead! Hit me!"

Shatz Abel began to laugh uncontrollably—and when he abruptly lunged up at Dalin, the king stumbled back, shouting, and sought to strike at the pirate in self-defense.

Shatz Abel easily warded off the blow, then grabbed Dalin's shovel from his hands and threw it after his own, into the storm.

"You're mad!" Dalin shouted in alarm, as Shatz Abel continued to laugh; now the insane man rose out of the snow, laughing, and lumbered forward to take the king in his grasp.

"Let me go, you lunatic! We're both going to die!"

"No!" Shatz Abel laughed. "We're both going to *live*!"

The pirate wrestled briefly with Dalin, turning him around in the direction of their habitat set within the side of a hill.

"Look!" Shatz Abel laughed.

Dalin stared; through a fog of snow, he could just make out the cleared-away entrance of their home.

"Don't you understand?" Shatz Abel laughed, as Dalin continued to stare.

Realization began to dawn on the king.

"I can *see* it!"

"Yes, young fool! You can see it! The storm is lessening! Soon it will stop, and we'll be on our way!"

Dalin pushed himself out of the pirate's grasp and jumped into the air, giving his own whoop of joy.

"Finally!" he shouted.

"Yes! Finally, Sire!"

While Shatz Abel stood laughing, Dalin scrambled off into the snow and began to search desperately.

"What are you doing?" the pirate laughed.

"The shovels!" Dalin shouted in mock desperation. "We'll need them to finish digging out our supplies!"

Two days later, surrounded by provisions in their habitat, with the crystal-clear sky of Pluto, SunOne hanging warmly in one corner, greeting them from their window, Shatz Abel was in a more somber mood as he outlined their plan for the fiftieth time.

On a crudely constructed map, the pirate eluci-
dated their difficulties. One X represented their present home; another, two feet away, represented
Tombaugh City. In between, there were tentative
sketches and much blank space.

"The trouble is, I just don't remember," Shatz Abel
said. "I wasn't exactly provided with a viewer and
satellite maps when they dropped me on this snowball. And there wasn't much to bother pirating during my years in that profession.

"So we have our eyes, and what equipment we
possess. A hundred kilos is a long stretch to do by
foot. I've had a long time to think about this trip,
Sire, and I'm afraid that's the way we have to go.
Ballooning is out; we need to go north and would
never get there with the wind always blowing west.
I've salvaged parts from two crashed satellites and a
downed shuttle over the years, but even a sled hits
difficulties twenty kilos or so out. Trouble is, the land
is just too rough for a spell. It gets very icy beyond
that, but it'll be impossible to get a sled past the
rough spots. The farthest I've gone myself is twenty-
two kilos, which took me three days there and back.
I saw enough in that time to know that once this trip
is committed to, there's no turning back."

He stabbed a thick finger at a smudge on the map,
a little ways from their home.

"That's as far as I got, laddie. A gorge that stopped
me cold. I think it's called Christy Chasm. You've
seen Vales Marinares, on Mars? Shrink it down, and
coat it with ice, and now you've got an idea."

"How far did you explore to either side? Maybe there's an ice bridge—"

Shatz Abel laughed. "Ice bridge? The monster is a kilometer wide, at least. We'll have to descend. And that's where things get ill-defined. . . ."

For the first time since Dalin had known him, the pirate showed not only doubt but a touch of something else—fear, almost.

"What is it?"

"It's not anything I've mentioned before, because it's more of a rumor than fact. But there are stories about Christy Chasm."

When the pirate merely frowned, Dalin said, "What kind of stories?"

Shatz Abel rose, rolled his map into one ham-sized fist and cried, "Bah! Best to forget it. I never was one for fairy tales myself."

Dalin stood his ground. "Tell me."

Looking flustered, Shatz Abel finally relented. "There's stories of goblins down there. Creatures of Pluto that were here before SunOne or any human, sheet-white things made of frost or fog that no one's ever seen. Or lived to tell about, anyways."

Dalin laughed. "The *boogey*man? Here?"

Shatz Abel frowned. "Best not to laugh about it, Sire."

Dalin laughed even harder. "There's nothing to do *but* laugh! If bogey stories are the most we have to contend with, I say let's start now!"

The pirate continued to frown, until Dalin Shar approached to slap him on the back.

"Look at us!" Dalin said with bluster. "Me the

fearless one and you the scared pup! Do we have a choice about making this trip, Shatz Abel?"

"Why, no . . ."

"Then why are we standing here making excuses for not going? We each have work to do! You want to get off Pluto as much as I, don't you?"

"Yes. But it's best not to make light of such stories—"

Dalin's enthusiasm flared to mild anger: *"Do we have a choice?"*

His resolve reinstated, Shatz Abel said, "No."

"Then let's get ready to leave!"

Filling his barrel chest with air, the pirate said, "Yes! Let's do that, then!"

Dalin laughed; and soon, as SunOne touched the horizon's mountains outside with twilight, they had resumed their packing, Shatz Abel singing a lusty pirate song with his nearly bottomless courage and enthusiasm renewed:

> "So keel-haul the blighter
> From cockpit to stern,
> And pillage that freighter—
> What we can't sell we'll burn!"

Dalin hummed along lustily; but in his heart a clutch of questions and new terrors were fighting for dominance: *Goblins? Boogeymen? No one's lived to tell about?*

And though he smiled and hummed and packed with enthusiasm, inside he said: *What next?*

*   *   *

When SunOne was rising again, they were ready to leave.

To the north, between two far mountain peaks, their destination glowed invitingly. It would be dawn there, too. In Tombaugh City there were real streets, and bustling people, and restaurants and shops. And shuttlecraft, and Tombaugh Port—from which, somehow, they would get off Pluto.

"Ready, Sire?" Shatz Abel shouted.

Taking his eyes from the northern horizon, Dalin surveyed their sledded gear, which, with SunOne's help, threw tall shadows on the cleared patch before their habitat, whose window was now dark for the first time since Dalin had arrived on Pluto.

He tried to feel something for this hovel cut out of a mountain, which had kept him alive and sheltered him for three years—but he felt very little, except the wish to be moving. He found himself turning to the sky, to once again search for tiny Earth in all those stars—

"All aboard, my liege! Ready to pull anchor!"

Dalin jumped onto Shatz Abel's sled, as long as five men and as wide as three, its runners of nearly frictionless sheathing cut from the skin of the abandoned shuttle. The sail, on a mast fashioned from the bow-mast of the same shuttle, now unfurled, with Shatz Abel's expert guidance, to its fully massive length and instantly caught the eight-mile-an-hour wind.

Immediately they slid forward, up the incline of their cleared hollow and onto the newer snow plains of the recent storm; and Shatz Abel, whooping from his position in the center of the sled, maneuvered the sail and turned them north.

"Away we go, my king! Away we go!"

Dalin shouted into the wind and looked back at the rapidly disappearing hill that had, up until a few moments ago, imprisoned him.

No wonder I feel nothing for it.

"Yes! Away!" he shouted.

"Ha ha!" the pirate answered, as they sped on.

Soon even their hill was lost to sight behind them, and Dalin knew that he had seen it for the last time.

They covered ten kilos by sled the first day, then tented a camp and covered the final twelve by midday the second. SunOne was high overhead, washing out stars to either side of it yet leaving a black corona of night sky at the horizon, when Shatz Abel lowered the sail and they coasted to a stop at the far edge of a level plain.

Before them, the land changed radically. What had been smooth snow became jagged gullies and sharp hillocks; but the far mountains seemed noticeably closer.

"Foothills of the Plutonian Apennines," Shatz Abel explained. "From now on it's rough and rougher, till we get to the mountains themselves. Luckily we get to pass between two of 'em across a valley. The others would surely kill us."

Dalin studied them with their single pair of ancient binoculars; they looked much as they had when he had dropped into the atmosphere courtesy of Wrath-Pei: like jagged teeth waiting to bite him.

"I supposed we'll see," Dalin said.

"That we will. If . . ."

He stopped himself and said, "Time to secure whatever gear we can't bring, and get ready for our trek tomorrow."

Overhead a moving dot of light caught Dalin's eye; it seemed to detach itself from SunOne and move off toward the distant mountains.

Shatz Abel said, "You've seen your first transport heading for Tombaugh City, my king. We're now close enough to pick them up as they drop. A good sign, no?"

Dalin nodded. "A good sign."

They worked, securing and camouflaging their gear, pitched camp again, and waiting for the next morning.

"Now we walk!" Shatz Abel said.

Dalin's pack felt as if he were carrying himself on his own back; but he said nothing, noting that the pirate's pack was twice the size of his own. The snow boots he wore seemed oversize, but he soon came to see their advantages, when they hit the first deep pool of drifted snow and the boots kept him from sinking as their webbed soles automatically widened.

"Look back!" Shatz Abel ordered, when they stopped to rest briefly an hour later.

Dalin looked behind them and was surprised to see that nothing looked familiar. It was as if they had dropped onto another planet; for the moment, at least, gone were the snow plains and familiar hills; the landscape in all directions looked more like ancient Mars after an infrequent snowfall, pocked with glazed boulders and rusty rocks.

"It gets even stranger ahead," Shatz Abel promised. "Ready?"

Dalin adjusted his pack and breathed deep. "Ready," he said.

They trudged on, snow dust gradually giving way to stretches of black, interspersed with lengthy patches of ice. Dalin's boots adjusted as well as they were able; on the ice, tiny spikes were activated, keeping him from falling; but once or twice, in the middle of black-red sand, his boots mistook this substance for snow and widened, nearly pitching Dalin over. He learned to trudge carefully.

But soon there was more ice than anything: a bluish plain swept with snow devils that twirled like dervishes around them. Cracks in the surface appeared, sometimes forming strange pictures; some looked like spider webs, or a Screen's interference patterns, or the tendrilous heart of a nebula's star-forming region. One looked like an Earth cow; another like a distorted human face.

"Dalin! Look out!"

The king was so absorbed in finding pictures that he nearly stepped into a crack wider than a man. His gripping boots stopped him and he looked down into dark blue nothingness as Shatz Abel reached his side.

The pirate shone a hand lantern down into the crevasse, but still they could see no bottom; to the contrary, the chasm seemed to widen out as it deepened.

"That would have been the end of you," the pirate said.

Dalin backed away, resolving to look at no more pictures in the ice.

They walked on.

The plain became as an ocean, as wide and far as the eye could see—save for something in the near distance, a disturbance or frozen roiling in the ice that became more pronounced as they approached it. Beyond, the ice flattened again to the northern horizon, until the jagged peaks of the Plutonian Apennines thrust up like ravenous fangs at the sky.

Pointing to the disturbance in the ice, Shatz Abel said, "Christy Chasm!"

And soon enough they reached it.

Dalin now understood the pirate's description: it did, indeed, resemble Screen pictures Dalin had seen of Mars's great canyon, Valles Marinares, which cut that planet nearly in half across a third of its circumference. Take the red tones from Valles Marinares, replace them with gray-blue ice, shrink it in scale for Pluto, and the two would be indistinguishable.

"How deep is it?" Dalin asked.

"I reckon nearly a kilometer," Shatz Abel said. "I wasn't about to descend by myself, last time I was here."

Dalin studied the length of the abyss, as well as its breadth, and said, "I understand what you meant now about no possibility of a bridge."

"It's just too wide, lad. We could spend a month trying to go around it or hoping for it to narrow out. Best just to go down and then go up."

Dalin nodded. "I agree. When?"

"Tomorrow morning, after a good long rest."

Again Dalin nodded.

Shatz Abel grinned. "Unless, of course, you'd like to go back."

"Still thinking of goblins?" Dalin asked.

But seeing the look on the pirate's face, as well as feeling the knot that formed in his own stomach, Dalin was sorry he'd opened his mouth.

"Best to get that rest, Sire," Shatz Abel said, subdued as he pulled their tent from his pack and began to erect it at the chasm's lip.

That night Dalin dreamed of something like white shadows in the wind, something that flapped before him before melting in the morning's daylight.

They began their descent at dawn.

There was an ice shelf fifty meters below their picked spot, and first they lowered their supplies down. Then Dalin prepared to go over the side, secured to a thick rope gripped in Shatz Abel's beefy hands.

"Now remember, boy, I'll let you down easy. Anything out of the ordinary, give a tug. Test the ice shelf before stepping onto it."

Dalin nodded, and in a moment Shatz Abel had lowered him into the yawning chasm.

Dalin looked down; through the glare of ice he saw the ice shelf, and the supplies piled on it, rising toward him. And then a trick of light, a glint or shimmer that floated like a wave between him and the pile of provisions—

Dalin yanked hard on the rope; immediately his progress stalled and he hung suspended in midair, staring hard at the spot where he had just seen the optical manifestation.

There was nothing there: the slight wind whistled coldly, pushing him askew; the day was bright with blue ice that hurt his eyes.

It was nothing.

"Boy! What's wrong?" came Shatz Abel's shout; and now the huge pirate's form appeared above him, holding the rope in one hand, as if Dalin were a marionette.

"Nothing!" Dalin shouted up. "Nothing's wrong—keep going!"

"Are you sure, Sire?"

"Yes!"

"Very well . . ."

Shatz Abel stepped back, and in a moment Dalin was lowered once more.

And almost immediately he saw the shimmer again: like a flapping mist that passed between himself and the ice shelf.

He almost tugged at the rope again, but refrained.

His body approached a section of the ice shelf just to the side of the gear; as he reached it, Dalin tugged on the rope to stop his progress, and tentatively tapped on the ice with his boot.

It seemed solid enough.

"Dalin!" Shatz Abel shouted.

"It's all right! Let me down all the way!"

The rope lowered, then went slack; Dalin removed it from his waist and now stood firmly on the ice ledge—

It crumbled beneath him.

Calling out, Dalin sought with his hands to grab at the still-solid ledge where the provisions were stacked; but the ice was slick, and he felt himself sliding down. He had a brief look below and saw nothing but chasm, slivers of broken ice tumbling into an endless hole.

He looked up and saw Shatz Abel's shocked face looking over the ledge above, his hand still gripping the slack, now-useless rope.

Dalin fell into nothingness.

And then was surrounded by a shimmering sheet of light, which seemed to float out of the walls of the chasm.

The goblin.

8

Of all the useless and unpleasant tasks Carter Frolich had to perform, his weekly audience with Prime Cornelian was the most irksome.

Though he always tried to control his anger and impatience, it always broke to the surface, to the detriment of everything he was trying to accomplish. Like it or not, he continued to need the High Leader; like it or not, his fate and the fate of his beautiful Venus were tied to the Martian warlord.

"Cornelian, how are you?" Frolich said to the High Leader's loathsome Screen image. Already having blundered, he sought to correct himself: "I mean of course, *High Leader*, how are you?"

"Well enough," the Martian said. He seemed preoccupied, as he often did—which was fine with Frolich.

"Are things well?" Frolich said, seeking to be diplomatic; the last thing he expected was a truthful answer.

"Not precisely, Frolich," the High Leader said. "There's been a coup of sorts on your home planet, Earth, and though it really was needed, it seems to have made things worse. And Wrath-Pei *vexes* me."

"Oh?" Frolich said politely, though he had absolutely no interest any longer in what went on on Earth. Venus was his home now—no, was his *life*; and only Venus's welfare concerned him.

"I was wondering, High Leader, if you've been able to consider my requests for that feeder tube upgrade project—"

With a wave of one metallic hand, Cornelian dismissed Frolich's concerns. "Not now. Perhaps next week. You don't have any trouble to report to me, do you?"

"Of course not."

"Good. Since the deactivation of half the Plasma Corps last month, I was concerned there might be . . . trouble."

Frolich had never seen the High Leader so preoccupied. To his diplomatically acute mind, it seemed the perfect time to ask for what he wanted.

"High Leader, do you think the power from the deactivation could be diverted to the Maat Mons plan—"

"Don't bother me with your toys!" the High Leader erupted.

"I'm sorr—"

The High Leader's quartz orbs stared straight into Frolich through the Screen. Through his anger, the High Leader spoke slowly and distinctly: "Just tell me plainly: are things quiet on Venus?"

"Yes."

"Good."

The Screen went mercifully blank, leaving Carter

Frolich staring at it for a moment, before all but forgetting that the High Leader had even spoken to him.

All that mattered was Venus.

Carter turned from the blank Screen to the rest of the cavernous chamber. It was the perfect place to work and dream: the Sacajawea Center's Piton Room, set four hundred feet high into the flank of the extinct volcano Sacajawea Patera like a jewel. It was an eagle's nest, jutting out nearly a hundred feet, its floor-to-ceiling windows overlooking a panorama out of Eden: Lake Clotho Tessera to the east, on its shores Lakshmi Planum, which would one day grow into a city; in the middle distance other communities, which, though disrupted in their growth, would one day prosper; and below, almost in the shadow of the volcano, was Frolich City, destined to be the planet's largest. It had been named over Carter's violent objections; briefly, he wondered if its former citizens, mostly dead now, would have argued so assiduously today in favor of that appellation. . . .

Bypassing the ranks of worktables holding architect's plans, stacks of engineering documents, miniature models of facilities—oxygenating stations, feeder tube plants, water purification terminals, transportation depots, and a hundred other projects and dreams—Carter walked to the edge of the Piton's jutting windows and surveyed this paradise he had done so much for.

Murdered so many for.

The thought drove briefly through his mind, but he pushed it aside. Yes, he had done what had been necessary to save his Venus; many had died in the process.

Targon Ramir's face rose briefly in his thoughts—
Murdered.

He drove Targon's face from his mind, just as he drove away all the other ugly acts *that had been necessary.*

What price is too much?

Staring out at the empty streets of Frolich City below him, where dust blew through empty streets and through backyards where children used to play—

The children gone, their parents murdered, cut down in their homes on Eden—

"That's not the way it was supposed to be!" Carter shouted suddenly, his voice echoing in the empty room. Here it came again: the attacks, the voices in his head, the screams, it seemed like the core of Venus itself screaming at him, calling him *murderer. . . .*

"*No!*"

Frolich fell to the floor, holding his head with his hands; if only the devils would leave him alone, the demons in his memory.

"*I had no other choice! You were going to kill my planet!*"

Targon Ramir's face, placid before death, his body battered by Prime Cornelian's torturers, his face stripped of flesh, bleeding like any martyr's, again came to haunt him. He had loved Targon Ramir like his own son, had shared his vision of Venus, of paradise, with this boy—and then Targon had betrayed him. Ramir had sought to destroy all they had

worked for together; would have blown up every
feeder tube on Venus, punching great brown plasma
explosion holes in its beautiful oxygenating atmosphere and sent the planet reeling back to its hellish
past for hundreds of years. . . .

"I couldn't let you do that, Targon!"

Unspeaking, Targon Ramir's ruined face regarded
him placidly, then faded away.

Through the floor's windows, Carter Frolich stared
wide-eyed at the dust-blown streets of Frolich City;
a line of plasma soldiers marched mindlessly by near
the city's feeder tube facility; the soldiers looked like
fire ants.

All the other cities, all empty, all full of dust.

Venus is no longer people.

If that was the way it must be, then so be it.

Slowly, Carter Frolich rose from the floor and
straightened his tunic. He turned his back on the
Piton's windows, walked unsteadily to the nearest
worktable. On it was a tiny, beautifully scaled model
of Aphrodite Port; fragile representations of freighters and transports were lined in a row on what
would be the largest port on the Five Worlds.

One section of the facility was still unfinished;
nearby were modeling materials, tiny sticks of plastic, a thin raser knife to cut them with.

Carter pulled up a chair, adjusted the lighting onto
the model, fitted a close-up lens over his eye for the
exquisitely delicate work.

He picked up the raser in his hand.

Regarding it for a moment, he pushed the tab that
activated the pencil-point-thin cutting beam.

Pushing up the sleeve of his tunic, he burned a straight line into his flesh, until he could smell his own corporeal self roasting, as he knew he would roast in hell when his time on Eden was finished.

There were many such lines on his arms, and thighs.

He had thought of burning his eyes out, but knew that he needed them for work and that his visions would nevertheless continue unabated.

His finger, rock steady, lifted from the raser's firing tab; for a moment he regarded the singed flesh, giving off a blackened smoke.

He let his tunic fall back over his arm.

He bent over the model, and began to work.

9

Remember.

Within the labyrinths of Kamath Clan's mind, withdrawal was beginning to take hold. She had always told herself, with the rock-hard certainty she held to all things in life, that if this moment ever came—as it inevitably would when Quog passed from life—she would be able to abide it. But she was wrong. Quog had become such an integral part of her existence over the years that now, when his essence was finally denied her, the depths of her addiction were all too apparent.

There had been other, shorter periods when she had been denied—or had tried to abstain. Denied: when Quog, in one of his periodic fits of temper or madness, had refused to see and provide her. Abstinence: when she had resolved, years ago, when it first became apparent that her reliance on Quog was becoming too strong—a danger for any ruler open to blackmail or extortion—to give up the pleasure altogether. Always she had returned to Quog and always, in the end, he had accommodated her.

It was only now that the bill was coming due, that

the danger in her failure at both denial and abstinence was all too apparent.

She both cursed herself for her weakness and
wished with all her being that Quog was here before her.

At this moment she would do anything he asked,
debase herself however he demanded, if only he
would furnish what she required.

What her withdrawing mind needed.

"Ohhhhhhhh."

Kamath Clan's head was on fire, felt as if the syn-
apses between her brain's cells were lit with hot
chemicals. None of her potions had eased the growing pain, the growing need; nothing she had done,
no mantra of Moral Guidance, no secular prayer of
her ancestor, Faran Clan, could remove this blight
from her mind.

Remember.

But she could not!

Her brain screamed for memories, for the sweet,
relived times on Earth, happiness under a sapphire-
blue sky, the bright-washed smell of a puppy wrig-
gling in her bosom, the towering safeness of her
mother and father standing against the warmth of a
perfect summer day; the nearness of Sol, hot on the
skin, the smell of cut green grass, and the gasp-
inducing stark wet look of a healthy apple tree
against that perfect sky on that *single perfect day.* . . .

"Ohhhhhhhhhh!"

But none of it came! None of it was there! While
her brain cried to relive that one perfect moment in
her life before everything became hard and changed

forever—that one, single, *perfect* instant when she
was six years old, the timeless frozen moment of
pure happiness that Quog had stretched out for her
all these years of unhappiness and hardness—there
was only fire! Heat instead of memories! Living
death instead of reliving!

Screaming out, holding her head as if it would
burst, Queen Kamath Clan fell to the floor in her
chambers and sought to drown her pain with blank-
ness. She would think of nothing.

But still her brain cried out for memories, sucking
at the dry teat of reliving!

Remember.

"Noooooooooooo!"

From far off, but only in the next room, she heard
her son Jamal undergoing his own pains. They would
not be as severe, she surmised—doubly for the reason that he had not partaken of Quog's offering as
long and had precious little of happiness to remember. Still, her heart, in the midst of the fire in her
head, went out to him.

And, in lesser measure, to the other. . . .

"Ohhhhhhhhhhh!"

The wave of withdrawal grew higher, carrying her
screaming with it, to the point, finally, where she
dove up into fiery blackness and lay still on her bare
floor, asleep but undreaming.

She awoke with the artificial light of day streaming
through the window. The Screen in her room proclaimed the time as midday. Her ordeal had lasted
days. She rose slowly, limbs trembling, from the floor

and beheld herself in the room's mirror; she was herself, only less so, a large figure whose outer skin had shrunk and wrinkled. The fire in her head had, for the moment, abated.

She examined the room, noting the scattered potion bottles, some shattered. There was a hole in one wall that she did not remember inflicting; the toilet smelled of vomit.

She straightened up, cleansed herself, changed her clothing, and, breathing deeply, went out into the hallway.

A guard stood back, looking fearful, but with measured relief on his countenance when Kamath Clan glared at him.

"You stood vigil the whole time?"

"Yes, my queen," he said.

She nodded, suppressing a shiver. "And the children?"

"Still in their rooms, my queen."

Kamath took an unsteady step forward, her glare hardening when the guard reached to help her.

"Stay at your post."

"Yes, my queen."

Kamath Clan opened the door to her son's room and entered, closing it behind her.

Jamal lay on his bed, mouth open wide, staring at something on the ceiling that wasn't there.

When Kamath stood over him, invoking his name, he said nothing, but his parched lips undertook to move.

In a cold whisper, Kamath said, "It will be all right,

Jamal. You are new to it, and I pray it will let you go more easily. Also, you will enjoy its benefits longer.''

Obviously lost in a mixture of pain and rapture, Jamal nodded almost imperceptibly.

"Ta-brel . . .''

Kamath said, "Yes. I will see her now.''

She left Jamal and opened the door separating her son's room from his inconsummate bride's.

Tabrel Kris, in a condition similar to Jamal's, sat huddled in a corner, eyes staring at nothingness.

"You are stronger than my son, and it will give you up less easily,'' Kamath Clan said. "Enjoy it while you can.''

The girl's lips moved, and the queen moved close enough to hear the word "garden'' spoken in a whisper.

"Be in your garden, then,'' Kamath Clan said; and then, in a gesture that in her normal course would have been abhorrent and alien to her, she touched the girl's head.

"Stay in your garden as long as you may, and fight with your nails to give it up.''

Briefly, and with a flicker of recognition, Tabrel looked up at her; and Kamath Clan, startled, saw defiance.

In a moment the waning drug overwhelmed her again, and her mouth moved ever so slightly.

"Garden . . .''

"Yes,'' Kamath said, all thoughts of tenderness purged, other thoughts of necessity overtaking them.

Suddenly she knew what must be done.

*   *   *

Back in her chambers, the queen activated her Screen and sought to call Wrath-Pei.

One last time.

Still, the traitorous pirate would not speak with her. The Screen remained blank, and Kamath Clan could almost hear Wrath-Pei's laughter.

She switched the Screen off.

An image of Quog—alive or dead, it made no difference—flashed before her, and she could feel the aching fire of withdrawal rising within her again.

"Damn you, Wrath-Pei."

He would laugh no more when she was finished with him.

Quickly, before her brain's burning became too much for her to bear and she collapsed screaming to the floor once more, she reactivated the Screen and placed another call, one she had never before made.

Before long she spoke with Prime Cornelian, High Leader of Mars.

10

Dalin was doomed—and then he was alive.

There was no other way to think of it. The sequence of events was a simple one: he had put his weight on the ice shelf; the shelf had given way, causing him to fall to his death; *something* had shimmered beneath him, and then he was back on the ice shelf, on a solid wide area beside all of his and Shatz Abel's equipment, as if nothing had happened.

It was that simple—and that complicated.

What had the *goblin*—the thing that saved him—been?

He had no idea; except that he had felt a tingle on his skin, as if something had penetrated him skin-deep. And then he had felt nothing, and the creature, whatever it had been, was gone.

He rolled up his sleeve and examined his skin; there was no trace of anything, and nothing unusual, no shimmer, no wave of light, was left anywhere around him.

By this time, Shatz Abel, nearly mad with concern, had made his way down to the ice ledge; he looked down for a safe place to step and his eyes widened with astonishment to see Dalin looking safely up at him.

"But Sire! I saw—I mean, you fell—I mean—"

"Yes, I did fall," Dalin said. "But here I am."

"Goblins!" Shatz Abel said, standing firmly now on the ice ledge. He reached out to poke at the king tentatively.

Dalin said, "Yes. Apparently there *are* goblins."

"I knew it! We're doomed!"

"Hardly," Dalin said. "After all, whatever it was, it saved my hide."

"True!" the pirate said. He edged to the ice shelf's lip and looked over. "Is it gone?"

"I think so," Dalin said. "When it let me go it seemed to melt upward, into thin air."

"*Goblins!* So the stories are true!"

"It looks that way," Dalin said. "Shouldn't we be moving on?"

Shatz Abel was studying the entire area around them, eyes darting to and fro.

"I said it's *gone*," Dalin said.

"Perhaps," the pirate said, looking at Dalin. "Then again, perhaps not."

Rather than stay on the inconstant ice shelf, they began their descent. Below them another hundred meters was a narrower shelf, and they climbed down to it. This time, Shatz Abel went first, driving pitons deep into the ice; they both wore harnesses and trusted no crevice or step.

Halfway to the next ledge the ice began to dissipate; and soon they were descending a sheer rock face. To Dalin's surprise, he saw that what he had taken to be bottomless had seemed so because the rock's deepening color had given the illusion of making it look deeper than it actually was. In fact, below the second ledge they soon reached a slope that angled downward into a long valley. Soon they were walking instead of rappelling.

When they rested, Dalin looked up to mark their progress and was astounded by how much territory they had covered; the black sky above was a faraway slit between towering walls of rock and ice. At the bottom, their valley had nearly evened out; at this rate, they would reach the far side before making camp and be ready to make the ascent up the far wall after sleep.

"It's not as bad as I thought it would be," Dalin said.

Shatz Abel shook his head. "As I keep telling you, Sire, we've barely started. And it's a lot harder to climb up than *fall* down."

The huge pirate began to study their surroundings closely as they walked; no doubt, Dalin thought, looking for goblins.

At the base of the far canyon wall, they camped, ate from food tubes and sought sleep. Dalin knew that Shatz Abel was having trouble with slumber— the big man snored like a bellows when he slept, and tonight there was only silence, punctuated by occasional loud snufflings, from the pirates's sleeping bag. Dalin himself found sleep elusive; here at the bottom of Christy Chasm the wind whistled and moaned, sounding like a cacophony of wailing ghosts. High above, through the cut of rocks that showed the sky, he saw part of an asterism that may have been the Big Dipper; to either side of it a wash of fainter stars brushed the night.

Knowing the pirate was awake, Dalin asked, "Shatz Abel?"

The other grunted, then said, "What is it?"

"Why isn't there snow down here?"

"The storm's are localized. There are times when this arroyo is filled to the brim with snow, I'll wager."

"Are you worrying about goblins?"

The pirate snorted. "Not worrying. Wondering."

"You have no idea what they are?"

"None. And it vexes me. I've been to most of the moons of the Solar System, set foot on every planet you could set foot on, and yet I've never met anything but transplanted men. We're all of us from Earth, your domain, originally; the Martians, Titanians, what men are left on Venus, here on Pluto. All from Earth. Outside of a few Martian fossils, there's never been anything anywhere else to compare with Earth life. But now . . ."

"Why does it bother you?"

"As I said, Sire—it makes me wonder."

Dalin was growing tired, felt his mind drifting toward slumber as he yawned the words: "Wonder about what, exactly?"

"Wonder about what's beyond our little Pluto here."

"Hmmmm." Dalin barely heard the pirate's final

words, and yet they penetrated his mind and colored his dreams with shimmers of particle waves.

"And who," Shatz Abel said.

Awakening refreshed and dream-riddled, they made their ascent by the light of SunOne.

Shatz Abel proved a skilled climber; and with their adequate gear they had climbed a quarter of the way up in no time. The spot they had chosen was not ideal, though, and now the difficult part of the mount ensued. Dalin was not keen on dangling from a jut of rock, held by rope and piton, while the pirate scaled above him, looking for proper hand- and foot-holds; one slip reminded him all too much of his recent brush with death, as he swung to and fro while the pirate, cursing above him, hauled him back to safety.

They rested in a scoop of rock face that could almost be called a cave; it drove back into the wall a good ten feet, but there was nothing of interest inside.

"Which is just as well," Shatz Abel said, "since there are other more mundane creatures like bats and such in these parts."

Dalin laughed. "What about your white bears? We haven't battled them yet!"

The pirate scowled. "You may get your chance, King Shar," he said.

Dalin laughed. "You fret too much."

After a meal and water, they proceeded; and, as SunOne was lipping the top of the far wall, where they had begun their traversal of the canyon the day before, they had nearly reached the top.

Breathing hard, Shatz Abel called down to Dalin, "I'll be going up and over now! Wait for my signal, then climb up after me!"

Dalin signaled him that he had heard.

The pirate, snugging his feet into footholds and using the piton he had just driven into the rock above him, hauled himself up and in a few moments had disappeared over the top.

Dalin thought he heard muffled words; he shouted "What?" and waited for an answer.

There came none.

But the rope was taut above him, so he proceeded to climb up after the pirate.

At the top, with a few feet to go, a shaggy hand reached over the ledge—without thought he reached up to grab it.

Nearly too late, he realized that this hand was in fact a paw, and now he looked up into the huge and ravenous white face of a bear.

Dalin ducked down as the creature swiped at his face; the curled claws caught and sliced through the top of his headgear, mercifully missing the head within. The animal roared—

—but suddenly it was flying out and over Dalin, into the abyss, its face filled with sudden shock.

Limbs flailing, roaring in rage, the huge animal dropped into Christy Chasm and was lost to sight.

"Sire—get up here!"

Shatz Abel sounded nearby overhead, and Dalin scrambled up the rock face obediently.

Peering over the top, he saw the pirate standing just in front of him, his back to Dalin; through the pirate's legs the king saw two more shaggy white monsters slowly advancing toward the pirate.

"I was able to push that first one over, but not these other two, I'm afraid!" Shatz Abel shouted.

Dalin crawled up between the pirate's legs, scrambling to stand up.

"Give me the weapon, Sire!" the pirate demanded.

Still on the ground, Dalin reached around for his pack and rummaged desperately through it; his gloved hands were too bulky, and he pulled one of the gloves off, driving his bare hand into the pack and pulling out what he thought was the telescoping staff they had packed; instead, he held in his hand a crude flare.

"Give me something! Quickly!" the pirate said.

Looking out through Shatz Abel's legs, Dalin saw the two bears mere yards away now, to either side. Their eyes were cold as Pluto itself.

The pirate reached down and Dalin thrust the flare into his hands.

"What's this? Well—fine, then!"

In a moment there was a blinding light; when Dalin pulled his shielding hand away from his eyes he saw the pirate, roaring like a bear himself, running after the two shaggy white creatures, which were shambling off, shaking their heads against the light that had momentarily blinded them.

The flare began to wear down.

"Dalin! Quickly! Run *that* way!"

Standing now, able to take in his surroundings for

the first time, Dalin looked in the indicated direction and saw a slope of what looked like ice, dropping off the rocky plain they presently inhabited, a hundred yards away.

"Run, damn you!" the pirate ordered.

Without question to the pirate or himself, Dalin sprinted toward the slope; when he looked back he saw the pirate hightailing after him, the two white bears with the sputtering flare at their feet, shaking their heads and just now locking their cleared vision on Shatz Abel. With a thunderous roar from each of their mouths they gave chase.

"Run, Sire, run!" Shatz Abel demanded.

Dalin continued to run, ignoring the huffing pain in his chest.

When he looked back once more, he was amazed and horrified to see that the bears had gained on Shatz Abel; their loping run had a terrible beauty to it.

"Ruuuuuun!"

Thirty yards from the icy slope, Dalin tripped and went down; when he pushed himself back to his feet, the pirate, running with all his might, had nearly reached him, with the furious bears close behind.

"When you reach the edge—jump!" the pirate ordered.

The bears snapping at their rumps, Dalin and Shatz Abel reached the end of the plateau and, with very little thought beyond momentary survival, jumped into what proved to be a deeper void than they had hoped.

They were airborne; and as Dalin glanced back, his

heart drove up into his throat: one of the bears had followed them over!

Eyes still locked on them, the bear hit the slope first, splaying its legs and landing as a ready-made sled. The other white creature had stopped at the edge above and stood glaring at the proceedings below.

With evident pain, Shatz Abel hit the ice, followed by Dalin, whose own rump absorbed some of the shock; immediately he began to try to control his flight, which proved impossible.

The plain was a pure sheet of ice, steeper than it had appeared from above; the three figures—man, boy, and bear—slid uncontrollably down, picking up speed.

Dalin peered desperately ahead; there was what seemed to be miles of ice to navigate before what looked like a growing tumble of rocks in the distance would stop their mad slide.

"Dalin—you must try to stay to the right!" Shatz Abel shouted.

Dalin glanced behind; the bear, far heavier than the two men combined, was picking up steady speed and gaining on them. Its ferocity seemed if anything to have increased.

The pirate bellowed, "Curl your body—like this!"

Dalin saw that the pirate had rolled partially onto his side, and was curling his body into a C.

"Do what I'm doing, boy!"

Dalin did as he was told; below them, the rocks drew closer, and the king now got the point: to the left, the rocks were coming sooner and looked more dangerous; if they could steer to the right, the slope ended more grandually.

Dalin felt something like breath on his back; he turned quickly to see the white bear just behind, raising a paw to strike at him!

Ducking low, Dalin curled himself into a tight C shape and the bear, unable to control himself, slowly slid past, staying to the left as the king and Shatz Abel moved incrementally right.

The bear flailed with vehemence, trying to slow himself down or turn himself in the human's direction—but before him the rocks inevitably loomed.

Dalin looked away as the huge white creature was driven off the ice into the field of boulders; there was a sickening thud and calling moan from the bear, which was then silent.

Far away, from the top of the ice plain, the bear's companion yowled.

"Never mind the damned bears, Sire—look out in front!"

Turning his attention to his own plight, Dalin saw that they were heading into their own boulder field; set in the ice like thrusting tablets were blocks of stone.

"Look out!" Shatz Abel yelled, as he and Dalin were split by a tall slab of rock.

They missed another and then another; and now the ice was thinning out—but the plain was thankfully evening out and they were coming to a stop.

Dalin lay on his back, panting, hardly believing that he was alive.

After a few moments the huge pirate, looking like

something of a bear himself, had pushed himself to his feet and stood looking down at the king.

Dalin rolled onto his stomach and tried to stand.

Shatz Abel threw back his head and laughed.

"My stars, boy!"

Dalin stood up, scowling. "What is it?"

The pirate held his sides, laughing.

"What's wrong with you?" Dalin demanded.

"Not me—*you!*"

Anger rose in the king at the pirate's continued laughter; Shatz Abel made a motion behind himself, patting his own rump.

"Look what you've done to yourself!"

Dalin reached behind—and discovered that there was no clothing anymore between his buttocks and the elements. It had been worn completely away by the ice, and his backside was sore to the touch.

Unable to stop laughing, the pirate turned, doubling over.

Now it was Dalin's turn to laugh.

Shatz Abel straightened; his face grew sober as he checked his own bottom.

"Heavens!"

"Ha!" Dalin said. "And you had *hair* to lose!"

The pirate made a painful sound as he touched his gluteus maximus gingerly.

"We'd best be covering our seats before they freeze," he said soberly.

Dalin, feeling the cold now himself, ceased in his own laughter.

Thus chastened, they sought patches, and coverings, and such.

*   *   *

It was not only their buttocks that had taken a beating in the slide. Though fortunate to be alive, and smart enough to realize it, they would now continue their journey with no provisions. Both of their packs had been torn open in the skid; everything had been driven from Shatz Abel's pack, and Dalin's held but one flap with two food tubes within. This would be the end of their sustenance; both of their water flasks had also been lost. Also, their meager instruments were gone, and their weapons. In addition, the backs of their boots had been scuffed to within a quarter inch of their soles within, and would not afford them the protection they had had.

Turning in a slow circle, then studying the sky, Shatz Abel finally professed, "We're in bad shape, but not out. That slide brought us a bit east of where we want to be."

He pointed to a dim green glow over a nearby hill.

"That's our direction, Sire, and we'd best be on our way, since hunger'll find us soon enough."

After a few deep breaths, they climbed the hill, which would be one of many they climbed that day, and the next.

On their fourth day out, they seemed no closer to the green glow that marked Tombaugh City. Behind them stood a flotilla of hills; before them, more hills, which led to a cradle between two mountain peaks. Above them, the sky was threatening again, an occasional blot of blowing cloud covering SunOne's weak light.

"I don't like this at all, boy," Shatz Abel said. He held up his own food tube, squeezed down to a quarter; it represented one-quarter of one normal meal. "And it's not so much the food as water—if only we could find water ice!"

He kicked at the dusting of methane snow that topped their present hill.

"Even if we found water ice, what would we do with it?" Dalin said. "How would we melt it?"

Shatz Abel grunted. "That's the easy part. You that spent your life in cushy surroundings don't know about such things—"

Dalin interrupted, "You mean the lens we lost on the ice plain? The one you'd use to focus SunOne's heat on, to melt the snow? Let's see, it would take you approximately—"

"That's enough, boy," Shatz Abel said ominously.

Dalin laughed, enjoying the man's anger.

The pirate held up his food tube. "You know, I could always eat *you*, Sire. You wouldn't make much of a meal, but it might be enough for one man to get along."

For a brief moment Dalin looked into the pirate's eyes and believed the man meant it—but then it was Shatz Abel's turn to laugh.

"Don't you worry, boy!" the huge pirate said, slapping Dalin on the back. "I gave up cannibalism years ago!"

And still laughing, leaving Dalin to wonder and then catch up, the pirate trudged on toward their goal.

*   *   *

And then the hills were gone.

"Will you look at that," Shatz Abel said in wonder.

Before them stood a frozen lake, a flat expanse of blue ice. They stood on a black beach; on the far side, over a jumble of low peaks, the glow of Tombaugh City was bright; they could just see the top of one tall spire.

"I'll bet that's water ice, Dalin. If we only we had our lens—and if only we had our sled now," Shatz Abel said. "We'd be over this in a matter of hours, and on our way. As it is . . ."

"As it is we walk, right?" Dalin said.

"Unless you'd like to build a sail on your belly and slide across on your sore backside?"

Dalin was scouring the nearby beach, looking for anything worthwhile to build a sled with. There was nothing; between the wind and storms and Pluto's dearth of surface vegetation, their surroundings were scoured clean.

Shatz Abel, already convinced of their plan, gingerly stepped onto the ice, testing its ability to support him.

"It seems thick enough."

"It should be," Dalin said. "The temperature never goes above freezing, does it?"

"It's happened, on occasion. A year after I was dropped here, SunOne went out of phase and heated the entire planet to a slushy mess." He seemed preoccupied, staring down at the ice with furrowed brows.

"More goblins?" Dalin inquired.

"No, Sire. But they do say there may be things

living beneath the waters on Pluto. Never seen it myself, but there was a fellow I knew, years ago, who did some business with Tombaugh City. Story was he had to land on one of the lakes and never took off after his repairs. Never found a trace of him."

Dalin was now ahead of the pirate, leaving the man to study the ice.

"Tell me about it later, in Tombaugh City."

The pirate nodded and soon caught up.

"It's not like we have a choice," he said.

Soon they were between shores. Hunger gnawed at Dalin's stomach; they had finished the last of their food tubes, and he banished thoughts of thirst by thinking about food. He tried to think about what it had been like before his food had come out of a tube; and since recalling the feasts he had had on Earth was too far removed from even his imagination at the moment, he concentrated on the finest dining he had done since his arrival on Pluto. There had been one meal in particular he remembered, something that purported to be carrots but instead tasted exactly like chocolate. . . .

"Hold it, Sire," Shatz Abel warned, halting their progress. Ordering Dalin to stay where he was, the pirate walked on, studying a heave in the ice.

After inspection he signaled Dalin forward, and they stood together, looking over a tall tumble of cracked ice blocks, which looked as though they had been blown up and out of the ice; around them the lake had refrozen, making a strange sculpture.

"Whatever did this was big," Shatz Abel said.

Dalin scoffed, "It's nothing but an ice fault."

They walked on, but the pirate shook his head. "There's more stories about this planet," he said. "About things they tried when they were building Tombaugh City. Something like the old yarns you hear about alligators in the Martian aqueducts—"

Dalin guffawed. "You mean those tall tales about pets being let loose when they got too big?"

The pirate retained his serious look. "It's all true!"

Dalin laughed even harder, forgetting his hunger and thirst.

"Laugh if you want," Shatz Abel said. "You laughed about the goblins. . . ."

Waving his hands in superstitious dismissal, the pirate walked on, away from the mound of ice blocks.

Dalin followed, his eye momentarily caught by what appeared to be a long black wiggle of movement under the ice.

"Shatz—" he began, then thought better of telling the pirate what he had seen; the man was superstitious as it was.

The king studied the ice, and again saw a long dark movement beneath them through the opaque blue; it slithered away from them and was gone.

Then the ice rumbled.

"What in hellation?" Shatz Abel shouted.

"I just saw—" Dalin began.

But then, before them, the ice broke upward in a mighty heave, and they beheld what Dalin had seen a glimpse of beneath it.

A long tendril, studded with jet-black suckers,

drove upward through the surface; it was followed by two more tentacles and the beginnings of a bulbous head.

"Sire—get back!" the pirate shouted, as a crack of lurching broken ice drove toward them.

They dove to either side, and Dalin watched as the monster's head broke from the surface, covered in dripping water; its flat red eyes regarded their surroundings while its tiny mouth made a horrible sucking sound.

With a mighty shudder the monster dropped back into the deep. A rush of falling ice dropped after it, and already the surface of the lake began to freeze back into place, monolithic chunks of ice forming a new frozen sculpture.

Shatz Abel was running toward the lately opened surface of the water.

"What are you doing?" Dalin shouted in alarm.

The pirate ignored him, and drove himself forward.

"Sire—water!"

Dalin saw the serpentine movement of a tentacle under the ice beneath him; he needed no other incentive to move and soon stood beside Shatz Abel, who had fallen to his knees and was scooping cold water into his mouth from the shrinking ice hole.

"Water!" Dalin shouted, and drank his fill before the ice battled his hands and the hole swelled shut with a thickening film of ice crystals.

The two men stood, panting.

"That tasted like liquid gold!" Shatz Abel said.

Dalin nodded.

In the near distance, there was another shudder of ice and two tentacles thrust up before dropping down again.

"Beginning to believe in tall tales, Sire?" Shatz Abel asked.

Wiping water from his mouth before it froze in place, Dalin said, "Yes."

A day later, further refreshed from two close-by water openings, they climbed the far shore of the lake and left it behind. Another series of hillocks led them to a broad, snow-swept valley—and then, suddenly, there in the distance was Tombaugh City.

"It looks huge!" Dalin said, studying the skyline.

The pirate laughed. "It's little more than an outpost! You've been living in the snow too long!"

What had appeared as a green glow from the distance now resolved itself into a brightly lit town bookended by two tall buildings. In between were a dotting of homes and lower structures; and, on the edge of the valley that separated them from the city, a port. As they watched, the needle-nosed shape of a freighter pulled upward in a burst of flame and was gone in a moment. Backdropping the city, hugging the horizon as if always on the rise, was the dark curve of Charon, Pluto's moon, half as big as the planet itself and locked in synchronous rotation around its parent.

Shatz Abel ignored Pluto's moon and pointed at the port. "*That's* how we get off Pluto," Shatz Abel said.

*   *   *

The valley, boulder-strewn and treacherous with ice and snow-covered craterlets, proved more difficult to negotiate than they thought it would. Once, Dalin had to pull Shatz Abel from Pluto's version of quicksand, a seemingly benign patch of snow that effectively hid a deep pit bottomed with icy slush. The king was able to keep his grasp on the big man and haul him out; after that mishap, their progress was even slower.

But, a day and a half later, marked by SunOne's stately warm progress above, they staggered, hungry and once again thirsty, to the fence that bordered Tombaugh's port.

This they circumvented, being careful not to be seen, and made their way into the city itself.

It was now that Tombaugh's bright lights, which had provided them with a beacon on their journey, proved to be a detriment. Their appearance, hungry, unshaven, dirty, bruised, and exhausted, not to mention without money, would have landed them in custody on the main street in a matter of moments. Shatz Abel was chagrined to see that Tombaugh was well patrolled by Wrath-Pei's forces. Though it made their task more difficult, it by no means made it impossible.

They kept to the shadows and darkened ways between buildings, waiting for an opportunity to present itself. They picked a spot in the center of town, amid the gambling spots and bars. It was now that Shatz Abel's confidence soared.

"Sire, I'm finally back in my element!" he crowed, looking happier than Dalin had even seen him.

And soon an opportunity did present itself, as a portly gentleman left the gambling establishment across the street and negotiated the icy main thoroughfare; he would pass right by their hiding place.

"A chicken ready for plucking," Shatz Abel said, rubbing his hands together.

Dalin took hold of his shoulder. "No! I won't have you assaulting a common citizen."

Shatz Abel turned on him with surprise. "What! How do you think we're going to get clothing and money?"

Dalin said, "Pick someone more . . . worthy of assault."

The pirate furrowed his brow. "In my business, Sire, *everyone's* worthy of assault!" he added, "Except for yourself, of course."

"Just find someone who deserves it more."

The pirate shook his head in resignation and watched in frustration as the fat gambler, singing to himself, waddled by their hiding place and moved safely on.

But, in a moment, the pirate's eyes glinted with pleasure at the sight of another pedestrian approaching.

"Well, I'll be . . ." The pirate chuckled.

"I thought I told you—" Dalin began.

"This one I know, Sire. And we'll need neither money nor clothing from him. But as for that meal I promised you . . ."

As the man passed them, Shatz Abel reached out a meaty fist and pulled him into the alley.

"Remember me, old friend?" Shatz Abel said, grinning into the man's startled face. For emphasis, the pirate lifted him so that the man's feet barely touched the ground.

"Why, *Shatz*! Shatz *Abel*! My friend! H-how h-have you been?" the man stammered, while trying to keep his feet on the ground.

"Not as well as you, Peyton, I'll fancy," the pirate said. "How is the restaurant business these days? Care to give an old friend a hearty meal—and whatever other help he asks for?"

"Of course!" the man said. "It's b-been a long time, Shatz Abel!"

"That it has," Shatz Abel growled, setting the man down. "And a debt is still a debt."

"Of course!" Peyton grinned, with a hopeful and strained look.

"And I've not forgotten your role in my capture," Shatz Abel said, causing the color to drain from the other man's face.

"Th-that was unav-voidable! Wrath-Pei—"

The pirate grabbed Peyton's tunic front up in his clenched fist, causing the proprietor to partially levitate once more.

"Don't mention Wrath-Pei in my presence again," Shatz Abel hissed. He brought his face to within inches of the other's.

"N-never!" Peyton stammered.

"Good." The pirate dropped the man back to his feet, but stood towering over him. "Now, this is what I want. . . ."

* * *

Twenty minutes later found Dalin and his pirate cohort seated in a back room at the most lavish table either had ever seen. Even in Dalin's court days he could not remember a meal so magnificent, from the Martian goose and Earth roast to the Titanian cheeses. There were wines from all four worlds, a new Plutonian beer with a distinctive flavor, and desserts from one of the finest bakers—a local man—that Dalin had ever come across. If he had still been on Earth and in power, he would have hired the man immediately.

"And now," Shatz Abel said, standing and belching, "I will attend to our accommodations."

"For the night?" Dalin asked languidly; he knew he would pay dearly later, after the years of lean living, for the rich meal he had just devoured—but he didn't care.

The pirate laughed. "No, my king! If we stay on this rock much longer we will be caught and dropped back in our ice cave in no time! There's nowhere to hide on Pluto—even for the night. We're leaving *now*!"

Dalin showed his obvious pleasure with a belch of his own. "Excellent!"

The pirate then left, meeting Peyton at the door to the back room and grabbing the man once more by the scruff of the neck—and leaving Dalin to the dregs of the wine and the crumbs of the desserts, which he proceeded to devour with relish.

And then, in no time—they were off Pluto!

In a whirlwind, Shatz Abel returned, grabbed

Dalin by the arm, causing him to drop the last bottle of beer, and dragged him through the restaurant, out the front door, and into the open door of a dark-windowed ground transport. In what seemed like no time at all they had reached their destination and were hurried from the transport straight into the open hatch of a freighter. Still groggy from both the speed of their escape and the quantity of wine and beer he had consumed, Dalin was barely strapped into his couch in the freighter's hold before the ship was thrown from its pad and shot straight up.

Blearily, Dalin turned to the nearby window and watched Pluto quickly recede, turning from a blue-white sheet of ice pocked by Tombaugh City and its environs—Dalin could just make out the valley between the mountains he and the pirate had traversed, and, beyond it, the hills and ice plain, before swirling dust and distance obscured the view—to a shiny marble circled by a dark moon half its size and SunOne, its artificial source of heat and light.

Yawning, he turned his sight from the window and lay back against the couch's headrest; he felt drowsiness overtaking him, and noticed how cosily *warm* the freighter's cabin was.

Sleep . . .

His eyes were half closed when a commotion up at the front of the freighter commanded his attention—it sounded like pots and pans were being thrown around.

"I said *now!*" Shatz Abel roared; there came mewling sounds of agreement—and then suddenly the hold's door was thrown open, revealing a grinning

Shatz Abel holding yet another prize by the scruff of the neck: a grizzled old man who looked very unhappy.

Behind the old man and pirate, muffled, precise voices sounded, and the old man turned angry for a moment, twisting around in the pirate's grasp to shout back into the cockpit: "Ye two hunks o' junk! I'll turn ye into aluminum foil, I will!"

Shatz Abel stood aside, still holding the old man, and Dalin was treated to a partial view of the ship's cockpit, manned by two confused and arguing robots.

Straining against the pirate's grip, the old man twisted around, trying to kick and punch at the nearest robot.

"Idiot! Tin shadrool! I'll trash ye!"

The pirate shook the old man, turning him around to face Dalin again. Shatz Abel grinned from ear to ear.

"Sire," the pirate said, "meet Captain Weems, who also owes me many favors." Addressing the captain, Shatz Abel continued, "I believe we were considering passage to Europa as partial payment, were we not?"

"Yes! Yes!" the captain said vigorously. "Whatever ye want, Abel! Ye an' th' sprite can go wherever this bucket'll take ye!"

"Sprite!" Shatz Abel said, in mock horror. "Is that any way to talk to Dalin Shar, King of Earth?"

Captain Weems started, then stared at Dalin for a moment. "Aye, it must be him at that. Though the way your sweetheart described ye to me, I'd be expecting more of a boy."

"You know Tabrel Kris?" Dalin said hopefully.

"Aye," Captain Weems said. "Transported your sweetheart once, three years ago, before Wrath-Pei got his evil hands on her. Tabrel Kris ..." He preened, which only managed to make him look even more grizzled. "Think she took a fancy to me, too." He looked meekly up at Shatz Abel. "I'll wager this'll strike us even—eh, Abel? Wi' the two o' ye as dangerous cargo, I mean?"

"We'll see, Weems," Shatz Abel said.

"That we will," Weems said. "That we will."

Behind Captain Weems, over the heads of the two robots piloting the ship up front, Dalin caught a brief glimpse of Pluto, now nothing more than a frozen blue dot.

11

The Machine Master was not a hard taskmaster, nor a cruel one, but he was difficult in many ways. He kept odd hours, paid attention neither to clock nor calendar, and considered meals annoyance rather than sustenance. He was sloppy in his dress, as well as in his work habits, did not take proper care of tools, and never put them in their place. Consequently, he spent much time in search of what he needed, and further energy on anger when he could not find it. In these areas, Visid was able to help him; but, though her organization reduced the amount of time the Machine Master spent in search, and seemingly lessened his anger at not having at hand that which he needed, it did not make him any more agreeable, nor less preoccupied. He was, in many ways, difficult. He never smiled; and levity was a virtue he considered vice. Preoccupation seemed his occupation. When involved with a problem he was anything but of the world; he was outside it, in another place, and could not be reached, even if the normal course of events demanded his attention. When the High Leader, especially, was in need of

him, the Machine Master was very often busy and
treated the Martian magnate like any courier boy or
common attendant. More than once, Visid had (from
her own hiding place) seen the High Leader's wrath
build to the point where it seemed he might swoop
down on the Machine Master with all of his metal
limbs clacking and crush or tear him to bits. And
though this had not happened, Visid felt that with
each audience the Machine Master, through his own
single-mindedness and inattention to anything but
his own concerns, walked a tightrope he might one
day fall from.

He was a difficult man.

And yet, Visid had never felt so alive as she had
since coming to assist the Machine Master. Her brain,
long used to attending to itself while the boredom of
rote Lessons went on outside it, felt on fire with ideas
and excitement. Her brain felt like a muscle being
flexed for the first time. From the very first day—
which she had spent in tasks as mundane as sweeping rat droppings from the corners of the Machine
Master's shop and pushing inches of dust, which fell
in cascades to the floor from old machines—she had
felt invigorated, alive, as she never had before. And
though the Machine Master spent neither that first
day, nor any subsequent day, in conversation with
her, she nevertheless felt the power of his presence as
well as his incrementally growing confidence in her.

When he needed a tool, she was there at his side,
bearing it; when his impatient mumblings indicated
that he was in want of a certain item of ancient

equipment, she knew its location and dragged it out to his side. And though in the beginning there was a tendency for her to get underfoot, which he proclaimed in freezing silence, her quick adaptability to his ways seemed to make a quick and permanent impression on him, and his silences became notes of approval.

"Visid, Screen three," he might mumble, and when she had rolled that instrument to him on its casters, leaving it beside him, his silence, punctuated by not so much as a grunt, led her to believe that she had done well.

As to his appearance: she had soon become accustomed to his ugliness and deformity; as comfortable with it as he seemed to be himself. His permanent smile, afforded by his snipped-away lips, and at first startling and horrible, became, in short time, merely his mouth. To Visid, in time, the Machine Master could look no other way. He sometimes spoke, often in sleep, when their long hours in the shop precluded proper quarters, and a cot might be erected near one of the damp walls, out of direct light from the high cuts that served as windows near the ceiling; and his speech was often in anger at Wrath-Pei, the benefactor of the Machine Master's appearance. The first of these episodes had greatly troubled Visid—she had briefly considered calling for assistance, until the Machine Master abruptly woke and rose, continuing his work as if nothing had happened. When it happened hence she knew that it was nothing to treat with alarm, only his way.

He *was* a difficult man.

And absolutely, of course, brilliant.

If this had been merely a damp basement occupied by a lunatic with instruments, Visid may quickly have tired of the novelty and sought release. But the things that the Machine Master turned his mind to were fascinating things to Visid. For the Machine Master's mind worked in fallow fields, churning up well-tilled soil and exposing treasures beneath. He took what others had cast aside, in both ideas and apparatus, and with the marriage of the two made something new—

—and useful.

"Visid, parts cabinet number five," the Machine Master said today (or was it night? the light drifting in through the high windows was indicative of either twilight or street light, she could not tell which).

Immediately Visid moved to a far corner of the shop and retrieved the requested part, an ancient computer chassis bursting with electronic components. Some parts had already been expropriated from the cabinet, but though the Machine Master had little idea where all of his components and tools resided, he knew *exactly* what parts he owned, and to what use they could be put. On the occasions when new machines arrived in the shop, borne by traders or confiscated by the High Leader (the Machine Master was not immune from asking for help when it was needed—though his asking so often sounded like demanding), Visid was amazed to see the Machine Master pulling covers from old parts, instantly cataloging what he now had at his disposal. He might never give that piece of apparatus another look—but he would know forever what it was composed of.

With a grunt—the cabinet was heavy—Visid set the requested piece down before the Machine Master and stepped back from the table. Without so much as a glance in her direction or a word of any kind, Sam-Sei proceeded to pull three tiny electronic components from their sockets, holding them up to the light for inspection before setting them down on the table and pushing parts cabinet number five aside. He then bent over a slim device, a hand controller of some sort, opened on the bench before him, pressing one of the components precisely into it.

Without being told, Visid retrieved the cabinet and brought it back to its place.

When she turned back to the Machine Master—

—he was gone.

And then he was back.

In a blink of an eye, nearly before Visid could react, the Machine Master once more activated the hand controller; there was a shimmer, during which Sam-Sei seemed to be surrounded briefly by a translucent egg, and then the Machine Master attained invisibility.

"Sir?" Visid called, but there was no answer.

Then the Machine Master was back in place, his huge eyes fixed on the device.

"It works, as far as it goes."

"Sir?" Visid said, unable to keep quiet.

The Machine Master turned from his project. "You have a question?"

"I . . . I . . ."

"I see. You are interested?"

"You were invisible."

"Not invisible. Transferred."

Visid kept silent, hoping he would continue.

"You recall the properties of the plasma generators, which drive the light soldiers?"

"Yes."

"You will recall, then, that there is a projector initially applied, followed by an amplification signal. It is a variation of the projector that is employed here. Instead of light we project . . . matter."

"Where . . ."

The Machine Master regarded her with something akin to amusement, though amid his placid demeanor and dreadful physical appearance it might go unnoticed to someone who had not worked as closely with him as Visid had. "Where did I go?"

"Yes," Visid whispered.

"Merely to the other hemisphere of Mars. The Utopia Planitia province, I think. It was rather cold, and they are having winter there at the moment."

Visid said nothing; and now the Machine Master turned back to his workbench, prying the cover from the hand controller to poke at its innards with a slim instrument.

"It is not yet suitable for my purposes," he said, either to himself or to Visid—she wasn't sure.

Taking a deep breath, Visid dared to ask, "And what are your purposes?"

He said nothing, but continued to work; after the

longest minute Visid had ever lived, he asked quietly, "Component board number eighteen, Visid."

She scrambled to get it for him, placed it gently on the workbench, and stood back.

He worked for an hour, during which Visid busied herself around the shop, wiping nascent moisture from machine cases, dusting, tracking down the occasional squeaking mouse to his hole and there laying a trap.

Another hour passed, and she was hungry, but said nothing. She was used to these conditions; during her free time, she was allowed her own putterings, in a far corner away from the Machine Master on an old workbench she had cleared for herself. She amused herself with an old intensity lamp, projecting white light through a scavenged prism to break it into its spectrum.

"Visid, come here, please," he called.

She looked up; the light slats in the ceiling were darkened with night. It might be four in the morning; it might be that a day had passed and they were heading into another night.

She went to the Machine Master's side.

On his workbench the hand controller lay open; many of the components that had been inside now lay in a scatter nearby. A rogue tool was clipped to a portion of the controller's innards.

Visid stood silent, waiting, while the Machine Master, seemingly having forgotten that he had summoned her, picked over a pile of slim, tiny old electronic components that resembled ruby spiders;

each was a garnet nub with delicate silver wires protruding.

Visid stood; and though her feet ached and her stomach growled for food, she said nothing.

The Machine Master continued his search—and then finally plucked from the pile a crimson part with a tiny green jewel embedded in its center.

This he put aside.

Still Visid waited for his orders.

He unclipped his tool from its place within the hand controller, lay it aside, and suddenly turned to Visid, his huge lidless eyes brimming with tears.

"Not suitable yet for my purposes," he said, choking within his lipless mouth.

"Sir?"

She reached out to touch him, but he recoiled from the possibility; his hands, which had laid flat on his lap, drew up to his breast and crossed there.

"I'm sorry, sir," Visid gasped.

He stared at her for the longest time, and then his gaze seemed to pass through her, to his previous thoughts.

"But soon it will be suitable," he said finally. "It will, you see, reach to Titan, or wherever Wrath-Pei hides at the moment. And we will have our long-postponed interview."

12

At Mel Sent's bidding they met beyond the Kuiper Belt, at the very outer reaches of the Solar System beyond even the Oort Cloud.

Since their last meeting, the traumatic one within the ring of cometoid material that was the Kuiper Belt, Kay Free had sought loneliness; indeed, if Mel Sent had not been so insistent now, she would have refused the meeting and stayed, a pale shimmer of light, facing away from the sun and out toward *there*. Only in this position could she hope to find solace, if not answers, to her questions.

And it was with a heavy heart that she met with the others today.

Mel Sent, uncharacteristically early, met her not with a greeting but with a characteristic shout of complaint.

"You would not be*lieve* what happened to Mother!" Mel Sent nearly shouted.

Pel Front, the last to arrive this day (it would be, it seemed to Kay Free, a decidedly *un*characteristic meeting), was greeted with the same announcement:

"Pel Front, You would not be*lieve* what happened to Mother!"

"I have no *wish* to believe what happened to your mother, Mel Sent," Pel Front said waspishly; it was obvious that he had been undergoing his own form of self-exile and, lacking Kay Free's politeness, felt no compulsion to be quiet about it. Kay Free did note that behind his peevishness there was the same weight of sadness that afflicted Kay Free.

Mel Sent, unburdened as she was by such feelings, waited impatiently for one of her companions to inquire what it was that had happened to Mother; in the interest of ending the present rendezvous as quickly as possible, Kay Free offered, "So tell us, Mel Sent—is Mother all right?"

"She *will* be, in time, I'm sure. The fact was, she was practically *frightened* out of her wits by one of the *creatures*."

Kay Free's interest was mildly pricked. She asked, "Where has she been staying?"

"On the farthest planet. The double one, with the weak light and the dry cold that Mother finds so pleasant."

"The one they call Pluto," Pel Front interjected, the snap of his tone conveying his continued impatience.

"Yes!" Mel Sent said.

"And what creature there did she encounter? One of the white bears? A mountain cat?"

"No! Not one of those—do you think I'd stir you from your self-indulgent mopings for that? A *creature*! One of the cognizant ones!"

Kay Free made what passed for an intake of breath with her kind. "A *human*?"

"Yes! The fragile, clumsy thing nearly fell on top of her! It was falling into an ice hole or something at the time—you know how vague Mother can be."

"And did she—" Kay Free began.

"Of course she touched it! She saved the wretched thing—what else could she do?"

"But did she—"

"Enter it—no! Do you think Mother's become senile?"

"There's been some question of that," Pel Front said sharply.

Mel Sent turned on him with similar sharpness: "She's not senile! And she acted properly. What's more, she said there was an . . . aura about this one."

Now Kay Free's interest was complete. She said, slowly and carefully, "What do you mean, Mel Sent?"

"I don't know, exactly; you know Mother and her ways of explaining things. She merely stated that there was something . . . special about this one. Yes— that's the term she used."

"Special . . ." Kay Free said. She looked at Pel Front, who was trying to hide his own excitement.

"There is a possibility . . . ?" Pel Front said, after a moment.

"Yes, it would explain much," Kay Free said.

"What are you talking about?" Mel Sent said. "You don't mean . . ."

Her two companions regarded her with an even

expression, and, after a moment, understanding blossomed fully within her.

"And to think it was Mother!" she said. "She will be thrilled; I must tell her—"

"Say nothing to her until we have a calling. There is nothing at all definite about this now," Kay Free said.

"And that decision is unanimous, is it not, Mel Sent?" Pel Front said harshly.

After a moment Mel Sent threw in the towel. "All right, I shall say nothing, for the moment. But if and when the calling comes regarding this, I shall rush off to Mother at the instant and tell her. Agreed?"

"Agreed," Kay Free said immediately, knowing that this was the best promise they were likely to get from Mel Sent. After a much longer pause, Pel Front also exclaimed, "Agreed."

"Good!" Mel Sent said. "Well, until the calling, then—good-bye!"

"We should wait, to see if it comes now," Kay Free said.

"But I have things to do! Places to go!" Mel Sent said. "And even though I can't tell Mother this news, I still have to attend to her needs, you know—she is old."

"Do what Kay Free says," Pel Front said, all traces of sarcasm gone.

Mel Sent huffed, then said, "Very well."

They waited; yet nothing happened; no calling came.

"There, you see?" Mel Sent said. And then, saying nothing more, she took her leave of them.

Pel Front, too, took his leave, after at least giving salutation.

"We'll meet again—soon, I hope."

"Yes," Kay Free said. "Soon, I hope."

Kay Free was alone.

But now, drifting on the very edge of what was allowed as her existence, in a place that shame and lack of understanding had driven her to, with her back to all she had been commanded to abide, she felt a new sense of possibility fill her.

She turned, briefly, to face Sol once more.

13

As had despots since time immemorial caught in a growing spiral of anarchy, Prime Minister Acron responded with the one thing he knew and understood: terror.

His was not a novel brand of terror—only the weaponry had been updated, and even that was new merely to Earth. After months of begging, Acron had finally convinced the High Leader that the only way to stop the growing revolt on Earth was to crush it with the same brutal finality that the High Leader had used himself when consolidating power on Mars.

"You mean you would use it on your own people?" the High Leader said, with what Acron took to be incredulity.

"Didn't you, High Leader?"

"Yes, of course. But I'm . . . *me*."

Acron had no idea if he was being made fun of by the insect creature on the Screen; he was ready to debase himself if that was what was needed to get the weaponry he craved.

The High Leader said lightly, "I see you have set

up a little map room—having fun with toy soldiers
and such?"

Acron turned, distracted, to see what the High
Leader was referring to: the room was, indeed, set
out as a war room, with numerous maps pinned to
tables, showing government advances and defeats.

The High Leader said, "There seem to be an awful
lot of black markers on your maps—I hope that's a
good color for you?"

"Rebel forces," Acron said, turning back to the
Screen. Willing his voice to hide impatience, he
added, "Please, High Leader. Give me the plasma
soldiers I request!"

"Out of the question. Once in your hands, you
could do with them whatever you wanted. And you
would have the technology to duplicate them—do
you think me a fool, Acron?"

Even with all the distance between them, the prime
minister still felt a tinge of fear in the pit of his stomach when facing the mechanical man. And while his
anger at not being addressed properly was in proportion to this fear, the fear, as always when dealing
with Cornelian, had great weight.

Prime Minister Acron said, "A concussion strike,
then. From the air. By your people."

Seeming to ignore the prime minister's request, the
High Leader said, "I've been mulling over our cot-
ton agreement, Acron. I think there's room for
improvement."

Instantly forgetting all pretense to diplomacy or
patience, Acron said, "Anything you wish, High
Leader. And about that concussion strike?"

The High Leader's metal countenance was unreadable, but after a moment he said, "That is a possibility."

"When—"

"I will think on it, Acron. I'll be in touch. Go back to your strategies, or whatever. Work on getting those little black markers off your maps."

With that, the Screen went blank, leaving the prime minister with the same mixture of rage and hope he had had before the conversation.

Only now he was able to show the rage, and turned roaring like a bull to smash his fist onto the nearest map table, sending markers of all colors, mostly black, flying, and a hole in the table and map where his fist struck.

Seated at a bench in a camp tent on a strip of land on the northern border of what had once, in the ancient days, been called Gabon, but which for the last two hundred years had been simply classified as part of the Lost Lands, Erik Peese had much to celebrate. By all accounts, his war with the usurper's government was going very well. Government forces had been defecting to his cause in growing numbers; and those that refused to cross lines were falling back on nearly every front. Many of the same local officials who had backed the plot to remove Dalin Shar from power had now reversed course; though Erik knew them to be nothing but cowards, sunshine patriots, he had long sought their political help as a tactical move. Now he had it, and more. The counterrevolution was like a stain spreading inward from the outer territories toward the centers of power, and it was only a matter of time now before so-called Prime Minister Acron and his traitorous cohorts were hoisted on a gallows rope. Acron himself had unwittingly aided Peese in his quest by murdering Besh; in one bloodthirsty knife thrust he had made himself known for what he was, a street brawler with no conscience and no plan other than to hold power. That Acron's power had almost immediately begun to erode had come as a surprise only to himself: his ministers, fearing their own futures, had immediately sought intermediaries between themselves and Peese's people, seeking to extend their own existences through further treachery. And once Acron's boat began to spring leaks, as it had, it was only a matter of time before it would sink under the weight of the fetid water it took in.

But, though Erik Peese had much to celebrate—especially in light of the fact that only a year ago, with the plodding Besh cementing his own hold on power through more traditionally brainy means; by, for instance, providing the commoners with bread and circuses, followed by more bread—he was not in a celebratory mood. For he knew that everything he had worked for these past five years, everything he had hoped to accomplish, had *sworn* to accomplish, could come to nothing if the butcher Acron was successful in obtaining his fellow butcher Prime Cornelian's terror weapons. Erik feared even the threat of those weapons—they had all seen the Screen views of the concussion bomb effects on the Martian city of Shlklovskii and of Earth's two former Moon colonies;

all three, after their respective attacks, looked as though they had been swept from existence. And Erik knew that his own fighters, dedicated and fierce as they were, would be no match for plasma soldiers.

Every province governor and local elected official they had made recent agreements with knew that, too—which only pointed to the fragility of those agreements.

So it was important that they regain power before Acron was able to convince the High Leader to employ his terror weapons on Earth—and it was just as important to return King Shar to Earth as soon as possible, especially now, according to reliable reports, that the king had effected his escape from exile on Pluto.

So much to think about. . . .

For a moment, Erik let his mind relax and thought back on that night three years before, when he had helped spirit Dalin Shar from his palace where death had awaited him—and how His Majesty had looked *dressed in women's clothing.* . . .

Erik laughed—and looked up from his bench to see his old friend Porto standing before him, regarding him with amusement.

"There! I knew it! There were wagers that you no longer know how to laugh, and I bet on you! And I won!" Porto said.

"You have news?" Erik said, letting his laughter relax into a smile.

Porto, ever the actor, struck a theatrical pose. "There is a possibility of a truce—with Acron!"

"What?"

"It's true! The vicious old windbag says he will meet with a representative of our 'government,' to discuss terms! He's packing it in!"

"Don't be too sure, Porto."

"What else could he want? He'll ask for safe passage off world, no doubt. He'll hide his miserable fat carcass on Titan and spend what money he's able to stuff into his tunic on information about assassination attempts. He's made enough enemies, that's for sure."

"True. And he's not the tactician we feared he was. But he'll be dangerous when cornered, Porto."

"Bah! He's ready to run, I tell you!"

"Then I'll speak with him."

Porto laughed. "You? That would be treasonous on your part! If something happens to you, everything we've worked for will fall down like a house of cards!"

"I'm just a man. We do what we do for the king."

"Of course! But where will he be when he returns if his new Faulkner is not here to greet him!"

"You honor me with Prime Minister Faulkner's memory, Porto."

"A great man! And so are you!"

"I'll go, nevertheless."

"Hogwash! You'll send me, and be done with it!"

Erik laughed. "You? What will you do—charm Acron with your tricks?"

Porto, to make his friend laugh, threw himself suddenly forward and boosted himself into the air, standing on his hands. He smiled at Peese upside down. "I'll juggle for him! Sing! Perhaps act out Macbeth—although he knows that one by heart, I'm afraid."

Erik could not stop laughing, as his friend pushed himself off of his hands and stood on his feet again, arms held out for applause, which Erik gave him by clapping his hands lightly together.

His face suddenly serious, Porto said, "I really think it should be I who go, Erik."

Growing sober himself, Peese said, "It will be very dangerous."

"I'll laugh my way through it!"

"Reluctantly, I agree with you. I'm more valuable here. The Ethiopian governor is due in, along with secret representatives from five other provinces. With the speed with which things are going, perhaps we should send no one, merely ignore Acron."

Porto said, "If we can end this one hour sooner, it could save another of our fighters' lives. And that would be worthwhile."

Erik sighed. "All right, Porto, you can go."

"I've already arranged passage!"

"I should have known." Erik stood and took his friend in a firm handshake.

"Return safely to us, my friend."

A smile split Porto's face. "How could I not, and give up the opportunity to make you laugh? And now," he said, slipping his hand from Erik and turning it into a bowing flourish, "I take my leave, and collect my winnings before striking the pavement with my humble feet."

"Return soon, Porto."

"Good-bye!"

At the tent's opening, Erik stood watching his old friend saunter away; Porto was unable merely to walk, but felt compelled to stop anyone he passed, to show a trick with a coin or to tell a joke. He inevitably left anyone he met laughing; as he strolled on, his recent contact inevitably continued to laugh, a day brightened by a small attention.

Porto soon drifted into the crowd at the center of the camp; for a few moments Erik regarded the sea of makeshift structures, made of discarded metal, found wood, and whatever else was on hand: blankets, rags, sticks. Many of these fighters had started with him when they had nothing; over the years, they had continued to have little but their own courage and the conviction of their cause. What had begun as a small band had grown to an army; and Erik knew they would follow him into hell if he asked. Even here in the Lost Lands, where the sky was tinged with a sickly yellow and rainwater was often undrinkable, laced as it was with acid; where game and crops were as hard to come by as breathable air—even here, they had followed him. If he told them they must drive even deeper into the Lost Lands, where mutant plant and animal life roamed unmolested, where the skies often darkened with tornado cones that ripped trenches through blasted soil—they would follow him there, too.

Off in the center of the milling camp, Erik heard a bleat of laughter and Porto's answering howl. He thought of the possibility of continuing without his old friend and discovered that he was tired of this

war and wanted only for it to end. Rather than see
Porto continually making a camp of warriors laugh
and sing, Erik wanted to see Porto where he had
once been so at home, and where he belonged—on
a stage. How long had it been since there had been
theater in the world?

Too long.

Wearily, Erik Peese turned back to his bench and
sat wearily down.

At the edge of his hearing, he heard another howl
of laughter, faraway in the camp, perhaps at the
outer pickets that led away.

"Be careful, old friend," he whispered.

14

Gilgesh Khan, ruler of no empire, was, nevertheless, descended from one. On the wall of his office on icy Europa, at the base of monstrous Carlton Cliff, was hung a duly signed and witnessed document containing a sliver of Lexan enclosing a minute particle of genetic material attesting to such fact that Gilgesh, mild and small, weak and inoffensive manager of the "Greatest Attraction in the Solar System," was, nevertheless, a direct descendant of the feared and hated Earth Khan known as Genghis. It was a matter of great pride to Gilgesh (it had cost enough), but it gave him no comfort on this day, when the ancestor himself might be needed.

"What in Rama's name could Wrath-Pei want with *me*?" he sputtered nervously, fussing with the instruments on his desk, turning to tap the tilt out of the framed and sealed genetic testimonial.

To his right, the side wall of his office was nothing short of a full window, giving a view of the lower portion of the cliff. As Gilgesh turned nervously toward it, a customer fell into view from the sheer icy white heights above, flailing as they all did until the autochute opened, bringing the rider up short a few meters from the ground. The rider kicked happily and touched down, running a few strides before turning back to gaze wonderingly at the wall he had just descaled. The trip down had taken nearly twelve minutes—an "Eternity of Thrills," as the advertisements spread over the Four Worlds so hyperbolically, and, nearly, accurately, claimed—and by the end the thrill seekers who took the plunge at the top were overwhelmed. It was a common reaction—and one Gilgesh had often wished he could charge extra for.

But such pecuniary thoughts were far from his mind today.

"Why *me*? Why *now*?" he whined, to no one in particular, being as the office was empty. On learning of the Titan tyrant's imminent arrival, he had sent his crew of four scrambling home, and prepared to close the attraction for the day.

There came a knock at the outer air lock, and Gilgesh for a moment froze, thinking that Wrath-Pei had already arrived. But that was impossible—the madman's ship had not yet been detected by Europa's sensors, and Wrath-Pei himself had declared that he would be extending his stay on sulfurous Io before traveling on to Gilgesh's humble amusement ride.

"There's nothing else *on* this frozen rock!" Gilgesh protested, before activating the lock on the outer door and running to the porthole to see who was there to waste his time.

Two figures shrouded in visored climate suits confronted him; the larger of the two began to raise a hand in greeting before Gilgesh cut him off.

"Go away! We're closed for the day!" he snapped.

The two, obviously stupid tourists, did not budge.

"Are you deaf? I said leave! Go to the hotel and sit by the fireplace! Spend money in the gift shop! Come back tomorrow!"

Still they stood staring at him, faces unseen.

A brief chill drew through Gilgesh Khan, making even his ancient Khan's blood freeze: could these two be advance guards for Wrath-Pei himself?

To find out: "Don't you know that Wrath-Pei is due here today? We're closed, I tell you!"

That got a reaction, and a good one, from the pair: instantly the larger one turned, pulling the shorter one after him, and they made their way out of the lock, leaving it open behind them.

Though secretly pleased at their alarmed reaction, Gilgesh was also angry:

"Stupid tourists! No discount for you tomorrow!" he shouted after them, activating the closing of the lock from where he stood. No one had any common courtesy anymore. . . .

But even as the lock closed, Gilgesh Khan turned from the door to fret once more over the items on his desk and to tap again at the ever-so-slightly askew testimonial on the wall behind his desk.

"Why *me*? Why *now*?"

Halfway between the icy beauty of the Europa Hotel and the precipitous majesty of the Carlton

Cliffs, Shatz Abel reached out a hand to stop Dalin Shar in his tracks.

"We don't have much time," Shatz Abel said grimly.

"Why?" Dalin answered. Though he couldn't see the pirate's eyes through the darkened visor, he nevertheless turned in the big man's direction. "And why didn't you ask Khan's help?" A note of sarcasm crept into the king's voice. "I thought you two were 'tight as tigers' in the old days."

Ignoring the king's tone, Shatz Abel answered, "We were tight, but Gilgesh is about as seaworthy as a sieve. If he knew we were here, Wrath-Pei would soon know it, too." The anger that surfaced when Shatz Abel articulated Wrath-Pei's name was evident.

"But what about his ship? I thought—"

"We'll have to stick with Weems a bit longer, as little as I like it," Shatz Abel said. "And the sooner we get to doing it, the sooner we get off this waste of a moon."

Without another word Shatz Abel turned toward the hotel once more; in a moment, Dalin Shar, throwing up his hands in resignation, followed.

Still fussing with his office bric-a-brac, Gilgesh Khan was startled to hear the audio monitor on his wall Screen come to life.

"Is anybody home?" a voice said lightly.

"Who is that?" Khan shouted back into the monitor; at the same time he ran to the window, straining to see up the sharp face of Carlton Cliff. "Don't you know the ride is closed? Get out of there immed—"

The last word turned into a gag in his throat as he caught a glimpse of a monstrous wedge-shaped ship, as long as Carlton Cliff was high, hovering over the top of the ridge.

Wrath-Pei's chuckle filtered through the Screen's audio. "Why, Khan! Is that any way to greet an old friend. Do come up and say hello."

"Yes, of course," Gilgesh croaked out. Already he was fumbling for his climate suit, climbing into it backward before discovering his mistake and pulling it off to try again.

All the while muttering, "Why *me*?"

The ride up was not pleasant for Gilgesh Khan.

The ride's owners had insisted that the elevator to carry customers to the cliff's summit not only be spacious but that it be nearly invisible. Made of quality quartz glass, the elevator was little more than a soap bubble in which its passengers felt as if they were riding on air.

Most customers loved it; but Gilgesh, being afraid not only of heights but of upward movement (two facts which he had judiciously kept from the owners, since he very much needed the job at the time) hated the elevator with a passion. This hate was only superseded by his loathing for the ride itself; he made sure that his hirelings did as much of the maintenance at the apex as possible, leaving Gilgesh to fret about the much more important matters of cash receipts and promotion—two endeavors that could be carried out very easily at ground level.

So tightly were his eyes closed, in fact, that Gilgesh did not even realize that the elevator had reached the top of the cliffs until he felt a gentle hand on his shoulder and snapped open his eyes to peer into the crystal-clear visor of Wrath-Pei's climate suit and see the delightedly smiling face of Wrath-Pei himself.

"Khan!" Wrath-Pei said, releasing the proprietor from his grip one uncurling finger at a time before settling back into his gyro chair. "So nice to see you again!"

As always, Wrath-Pei was dressed with impeccable, if chilling, taste: his climate suit, jet-black, was form fitting and seamless to the tips of his gloves; his helmet, save for the clear faceplate, was ebony also, and sculpted to mimic Wrath-Pei's swept-back lionine mane of silver hair. The effect was startling.

Trying not to shiver, and trying most of all not to stare at the holster secured at the side of Wrath-Pei's gyro chair like a scabbard, Khan bowed at the waist and stuttered, "And n-nice to s-see you, t-too, Your G-G-Grace!"

Wrath-Pei clapped his hands in delight. His protégé Lawrence, standing a few paces behind the chair, took a tentative, creaking step forward before resuming his silent position. Gilgesh noted that the boy was somewhat shorter than at their last meeting; bile churned from his stomach into his throat when he saw the blunt lines at the boy's thighs that delineated real flesh from artificial limb.

"H-how may I serve you, Your Grace?" Gilgesh Khan said, wanting only for the interview to be over.

Wrath-Pei, still immersed in delight, turned his eyes from Gilgesh to take in the land- and skyscape around him. Hypnotized like a cobra, Khan's eyes followed. Beyond the profile of Wrath-Pei's ship, outlined against the diamond-on-black-velvet of starry space, sat Jupiter like a fat red pumpkin. The horrid crimson swirls of its Great Red Spot were just heaving into view, surrounded by a thousand other variegated storms and fault lines. At the horizon, the contrast of ebon space with white ice was startling; a far line of cliffs smaller than Carlton stood like blunt teeth biting at the deep heavens. There had been vague talk about developing those other cliffs into further amusement rides, or the possibility of the exploitation of Europa's huge ocean, sixty feet below the icy surface. . . .

Suddenly Gilgesh Khan was filled with excitement: could this be why Wrath-Pei was here? Could this be about *money*?

Gilgesh's confidence replaced his fear in an instant. Now he was on terra firma. If there was cash to be made, Khan would be involved. Perhaps Wrath-Pei had taken over the present ride and had come to introduce himself as the new owner. Or perhaps he really was here to present new plans—for new amusement rides, a new hotel, even a theme park! Oh, joy! Oh, *money*!

"Your Grace, you are here—"

"I am here for two reasons" Wrath-Pei said, with sudden detachment. The tyrant's sight had fallen and stayed on the line of autochutes lined like obedient dogs at the edge of Carlton cliff. Beside them was the tall credit machine, the lone sentry of commerce, which allowed customers to release one of the chutes from its locked mooring, don it, and leap from the titanium ledge perched like a pirate ship's plank against the top of the cliff. Exactly eleven-point-eight minutes later the chute would automatically activate, ending the ride.

"Is it . . . fun?" Wrath-Pei asked idly.

"I wouldn't know, Your Grace," Gilgesh said, impatient to discuss the tyrant's plans and reasons. "I've never been down."

"No?" Wrath-Pei said, turning to study Khan.

"As to your reasons—"

"Yes, my reasons for being here," Wrath-Pei said. "As I said, there are two. First and foremost, I need this ice ball as a defensive station against Prime Cornelian. I am therefore claiming it in the name of . . . me, and closing your facility, including the hotel, forthwith."

Shock replaced both fear and anticipation in Gilgesh Khan. "But Your Grace—"

"Second, and also important, I am looking for an old friend of yours, Shatz Abel, who I'm sure has come to you for help."

Gilgesh Khan, dumbfounded, and beginning to feel fear again, sputtered, "I have not seen—"

"I'm sure he has come to you. I know he is on Europa, and there is nowhere else for him to go. He had an impudent pup who fancies himself king of Earth with him."

"Dalin Shar?" Khan said in wonder.

"Yes. When did they come to see you?"

"But they have not been here! They have not—"

"In the old days," Wrath-Pei said, "I overlooked your alliance with Shatz Abel because it did not matter. Suddenly it matters."

"But I assure you—"

"Lawrence," Wrath-Pei said, turning slightly in his seat to confront his ward, "please secure an autochute for Khan."

Walking like a man on stilts, the young man went to the credit machine; in a moment there was a loud click, and one of the autochutes unsnicked from its mooring and flipped onto the ice, waiting.

Wrath-Pei looked at the chute. "Put it on, Khan."

Gilgesh, quaking with fear, said, "Your Grace, I implore you!"

"Don't implore. Just do what I say."

Trembling, Gilgesh retrieved the autochute and secured it, pulling the straps tight across his front. It occurred to him that though he had helped countless foolish tourists with this procedure, this was the first time he had ever actually mounted one of the devices himself.

"Now jump," Wrath-Pei said, indicating the titanium plank jutting out into nothingness.

"I cannot!"

"Of course you can, Khan," Wrath-Pei said.

In a moment the tyrant's chair had whirred into motion, and Wrath-Pei hovered beside Khan, at eye level. A gentle hand was once again placed on his shoulder, urging him forward.

"Jump," Wrath-Pei said.

"I canno—"

The murderously cold look on Wrath-Pei's face spurred Khan into action, and he stumbled forward, moaning, to the plank's beginning, and then, step by edging step, to its end, where all of Europa seemed to hang below him in dizzying white splendor.

"Ohhhhhhhh . . ."

"Now jump."

After giving Wrath-Pei the briefest look, Gilgesh Khan did so.

He fell, into splendid nothingness—

—and found, to his amazement, that his vertigo was gone!

A thrilling ecstasy filled Gilgesh Khan. Behind him, the vertical face of Carlton Cliffs glided slowly past, as if in a dream. The wall was pocked with ridges and icy depressions that resolved themselves into pictures. Gilgesh had sold 3-D Screen views of these anomalies, but had never appreciated their beauty: the Smiling Clown, its face naturally etched in ice, the Rocket, a natural formation in the shape of a Martian cruiser, the infant, and all the others.

And here now were other marks on the ice—man-made graffiti etched by clever parachutists working vertically in a deft fight against gravity: "Mark Loves Ang-Frei," "Choi Lives!" and "Lem-Jarn Was Here."

As mesmerized as he was by his slow-motion fall, Gilgesh turned to face away from the cliff.

He felt suspended in space. There was the Europa Hotel in the distance, its green spires rising like emerald fingers from a blanket of white ice. And beyond it, all of Europa outlined now against the massive limb of Father Jupiter, King of Planets, its red, orange, and cream bands like a dream in the sky!

How could he have missed this wonderful attraction, this marvelous ride, for so long?

Each day, from now on, he would begin with a ride down Carlton Cliff, the "Greatest Attraction in the Solar System," to renew his sense of wonder!

And now Gilgesh looked down and saw the ground rising slowly up to meet him. How long had it been? Six minutes? Eight? In only a matter of minutes now he would reach bottom, the slow journey down nevertheless having imparted enough velocity to his mass to crush him like an egg but for the opening of his chute—

His chute—

It was now that Gilgesh Khan, long-separated descendant of Genghis Khan, who had proof of that blood bond, remembered what he had seen in that last brief glimpse back at Wrath-Pei before he had leaped.

What had he seen:

Wrath-Pei, resheathing his razor-sharp snips in their holster next to his chair.

And, in Wrath-Pei's other hand, the severed straps of Gilgesh's autochute; while, on the ground, the packed mass of the chute itself lay unrolling.

To confirm his fate, Gilgesh Khan reached around to feel nothing strapped to his back.

The flat shelf of ice at the bottom of Carlton Cliff rose inevitably up.

Gilgesh opened his mouth to scream—but something far down and ancient in his genes stayed his terror and steeled him.

He glared at the approaching ground with defiance.

And Gilgesh Khan, ruler of no empire save his approaching death, opened his arms wide to meet it as that other Khan would have.

15

The hotel desk clerk cowered beneath Shatz Abel's towering, rage-filled form.

"He *what*?" The pirate bellowed, as the frightened clerk tried to meekly wave something up at him from where he crouched behind his desk.

"C-c-captain Weems said to give this to you, sir," the clerk said, thrusting a data card up at Shatz Abel; the pirate's rage was only intensified when he saw that the hotel bill was attached to the card.

"That *worm*!" Shatz Abel fumed, but the clerk had already skittered away on all fours, as Dalin Shar tried to pull the pirate away from the desk and calm him down.

"Don't you realize we're surrounded by Wrath-Pei's men?" Dalin whispered fiercely in the freebooter's ear; already, two of the black-leather-clad figures, clustered at the small bar across the lobby, had glanced their way, and Dalin was certain they would be recognized if Shatz Abel's antics continued. It was hard enough for Dalin to keep his hood over his eyes. "At least let's see what Weems has to say," Dalin continued, pulling the pirate away from the desk and toward the nearest lift tube.

The pirate followed, and in a moment they had risen to their floor and were safely inside their room. The view, as was that of every room in the resort, was of the sheer beauty of Carlton Cliff. Even from this distance Dalin could see that there was some commotion at the top of the precipice—and, nearly dwarfing the attraction, was the magnificent, mammoth wedge of Wrath-Pei's ship, which hung over the cliff like a looming predator.

Shatz Abel was cursing, fumbling with the data card, which would not go into the Screen under his direction.

Dalin gently took the card and slipped it into the Screen's slot, then stepped back to watch.

A harried-looking Captain Weems came into the picture; he had obviously made the recording in one of the lobby's private booths; the trouble was that the booth was not all that private, and occasionally a figure passed close behind the captain, causing him to flinch and lurch into a sudden whisper. Flanking him was one of his robot navigators.

"Can't talk long, lads," the captain said, leaning closer to the recording Screen's lens, as if in confidence. "Got to haul m'self out o' here, if you catch my drift! Wish I could help ye further, but I've gotten wind at the tavern tha' things are gonna get mighty hot around here, and very soon!"

A figure passed close behind the captain, who was startled to the point that he nearly lost his voice.

Leaning even closer to the Screen, he whispered, "Truth is, they've already been checking all th' ships out o' Tombaugh Port, and if I try to get you lads off Europa they'll get you f' sure. So I'm headin' out now, and wishin' ye all the luck in th' world."

He turned as if finished, but then pushed his face back at the Screen. He said, hopefully, "Oh, and I imagine this squares it b'tween us, Shatz?"

"*Squares it?*" Shatz Abel raged. "If you were here, Weems, I'd square your head with my fists!" He made a threatening motion at the Screen, which showed the captain reaching for the data card while cursing at his robot navigator. Then the message ended.

"That's it, lad," Shatz Abel said. "There isn't another ship out of this ice rock except the shuttle back to Titan. And Titan's the last place we want to be at the moment." Noting Dalin's expression, Shatz Abel's demeanor softened. "I know how you feel about that gal, but there's just no way to do her any good by going to Titan at the moment. We've got to get you back to Earth. Titan and Mars are going to go at it soon, and when they do, we'll have our chance to get Earth back in the good fight."

When Dalin said nothing, the pirate said kindly, "We've been over it a hundred times, boy. There's just no other way."

"I know that," Dalin said. "I know what has to be done. It's just that every time I think of her suffering on Titan. . . ."

The pirate put a meaty arm around the king's shoulder. "You'll get your chance, Sire. I promise you that. . . ."

The freebooter's voice had trailed off, and Dalin saw that the man's eyes were locked on Wrath-Pei's ship, hovering like a black specter above Carlton Cliff.

A smile had begun to spread over Shatz Abel's face, and Dalin suddenly realized what was going through the pirate's mind.

"You're not thinking ..." Dalin said in alarm.

"Not thinking at all, boy. *Planning*."

"I've been on that ship, and I don't want to be on it again," Dalin said, but the pirate was already laughing, and in another twenty minutes had the two of them heading back down to the lobby in the lift tube, on their way to the bar.

They had their first drink alone, shadowed at a corner table, while Shatz Abel checked the possibilities.

There seemed to be plenty of what the pirate required: drunken men from Wrath-Pei's ship. Like any buccaneers hitting port, they were making the most of their time on leave, and in no time at all Shatz Abel had located two who would suit their purposes perfectly.

Three rounds of drinks later (the last bought by the black-clad soldiers), Shatz Abel and Dalin were trading war stories with the two men, after drawing them off into the same shadowed corner; it was as if they had known one another forever.

"So then the Old Man says, 'Time for a trim,' and off they go!" the smaller of the two said, roaring with laughter; to emphasize his point, he hoisted his right leg up onto the table, showing them all a view of his black leather boot, shortened to accommodate his lack of toes.

"Awww, that ain't nothing!" his companion growled amiably, displaying his two arms, artificial from the elbows down. "Did this in a fit of pique, he did," the man laughed. "Hell—all I did was turn the wrong valve and mix a little sewage with the ship's wash water!"

His friend rocked with laughter. "Hate to think what he'd do if you ever crossed him again!"

"Prob'ly cut my head off!" the second soldier howled, slapping his artificial hands together with a metallic sound.

"Snip, snip!" his friend mimicked, making his fingers into a mock scissors.

Shatz Abel laughed as loud as the two soldiers and pushed another round of drinks into their hands. Dalin continued to laugh but stayed out of the light.

"So what is it you boys do on Wrath-Pei's ship?" Shatz Abel queried in a friendly tone.

"We're *waste* men," the taller soldier said proudly.

"Yeah, without us—and we're our whole department—nothing'd keep moving on that boat. We manage all the waste and sewage. You might say—"

"Yeah," his friend said, completing what was obviously an old joke between them, "You might say that without us, things'd get *backed up*!"

The two of them burst into gales of laughter, which Dalin and Shatz Abel joined.

"And where are you heading next?" Shatz Abel asked innocently, a friendly arm around each of the drunk soldiers.

"Ganymede!" the shorter one said in disgust. "There's nothing there but a shuttle post, and some

Martian freighters the Old Man wants—not even a tavern!"

The other one said, "Yeah, and we'd best be drinking as much as we can now; when the shooting starts, we won't have another shot at it till Prime Cornelian is licking the Old Man's boots."

"Won't *that* be something to see—the Old Man and Cornelian! He'll have to sharpen those blades if he wants to take a cut or two out of the Bug, let me tell you!"

They all laughed, and the short soldier made his fingers into scissors once more.

"Snip! Snip!"

"Say . . ." Shatz Abel said, as if he had just been struck with a wonderful idea. "Have you two ever seen some of Wrath-Pei's *best* work?"

"What do you mean?" the short soldier said.

His friend shivered. "I hope you don't mean that little crawly fellow the Old Man keeps around."

"*Lawrence.*" The first soldier shivered also, and drained his glass.

"No, I mean the *best*," Shatz Abel whispered. Then he pointed to Dalin, who leaned forward partially into the light to reveal his lidless eyes.

"Don't look so special to me," the short soldier said; he examined his empty glass.

"Oh," Shatz Abel promised, "what you see is only part of what makes this boy special. And I've got a bottle of something special up in our room, too."

"A bottle?" the short soldier asked.

Shatz Abel grinned. "And not the cheap rotgut they serve in here, either. I'm talking *Earth* brandy."

The two soldiers' mouths dropped open.

"*Earth* brandy?" the short one said in wonder. "I haven't ever *seen* a bottle of it, never mind tasted it."

Shatz Abel had already maneuvered the two soldiers from their chairs and was steering them out of the bar toward the lift tube.

"Oh, you'll taste it, all right," he promised.

The taller soldier stopped dead as they were entering the lift tube and turned to Dalin, who had been trailing behind them.

"Hey, what *did* the Old Man clip on the little fellow here, eh?"

Shatz Abel, laughing, leaned over and whispered something in the man's ear; in a moment he was laughing, leaning into his friend to pass along his new information in a whisper.

"No fooling?" the shorter soldier said, guffawing. As the lift tube closed on them, they turned in unison to stare at Dalin, who stood stoically as they laughed at him.

"Imagine that," the tall one said, and the two of them broke into laughter again.

In less than twenty minutes the two soldiers, removed of their black clothing, identification cards, weapons, and money, lay trussed in the hotel room's bathroom, back to back in the empty tub, the hotel bill laid neatly nearby, and Dalin and Shatz Abel, this time in reasonably well-fitting garb (though Dalin was having trouble with the shorter soldier's truncated boot) were on their way with all official speed to Wrath-Pei's ship. They were surprised to find their transport packed with black-clad soldiers; without trouble, they were able to learn that a general recall had been ordered.

"And I hear we're pulling out within the hour," a soldier near Shatz Abel and Dalin said to another.

"That means the Old Man must have finished his business here already," the other said, and there was laughter.

But an hour later they were not on their way to Ganymede. Dalin and his pirate friend—hiding in a supply closet because, in the confusion of quick departure, they could not locate the area where the soldiers they had replaced were stationed—learned to Shatz Abel's anger and Dalin Shar's secret elation that they were on their way, with all due speed, to Titan.

16

Of all the times that Pynthas Rei dreaded facing the High Leader—and that included *every* time—the Period of Darkness was by far the worst.

It was not that the High Leader was in a foul mood to begin with during this Period of Darkness—to the contrary, it was, for him, a time of relative peace and contentment. That would soon change, of course, with the news that Pynthas bore. It was, rather, the Period of Darkness itself that gave Pynthas the shivers. The former Prime Cornelian had many odd habits and customs necessary to his station and circumstance; but of all of them, the Period of Bathing (merely repulsive to Pynthas's eye), the Period of Clinging (during which the High Leader crawled to the ceiling of his chambers and clung there, upside down, like any common house spider—the High Leader claimed it restored precious lubricant to the upper sections of his metallic carapace and the outer reaches of his limbs), and all the others, the Period of Darkness was, to Pynthas, the oddest and most unsettling of all.

There was a separate chamber for the Period of

Darkness, and now, as Pynthas Rei stood outside its door, he sought to find any reason at all why he should not enter. For inside . . .

"Pynthas, is that you? I can see you, you know, you fool."

Pynthas Rei had, as usual, overlooked an important detail; he now looked up at the tiny lens of the security camera over the door and tried to smile.

"H-h-hello, High L-leader."

"Come in. And bring the data card you're clutching with you."

The High Leader's languid voice belied the irritation it held.

"Y-yes, H-high—"

The door opened, and, like a mongoose mesmerized by a cobra, Pynthas Rei entered.

The door immediately closed behind him, and Pynthas found himself in total darkness. His hands had become so moist with discomfort that the data card he bore slipped from his fingers to the floor.

"Ohhhhhh," Pynthas moaned, but the High Leader merely laughed torpidly.

"Find it, you fool."

Pynthas immediately dropped to all fours, patting at the cold stone floor, but was unable to locate the card.

A long sigh escaped from the High Leader, and Pynthas felt him draw near; in a moment he looked up and gasped to see the High Leader's two vertically shaped eyes, like cobalt-blue cat's eyes, glowing not a foot away from his face; back there somewhere he discerned his own reflection, and now he felt the High Leader's hot, oily breath break over his face.

"Fiiiind iiiiit," the High Leader said in a languid hiss.

"Yes, High Leader! Immediately!"

"You're ruining my Period of Darkness, Pynthas," the High Leader warned, and now Pynthas Rei knew this was true, because the High Leader's wound-down mechanisms began to hum back to life, bringing the High Leader back up from his level of turpitude to his dangerously explosive self.

"Does thissss . . . *help?*" the High Leader screamed, rising back to full working level as the lights in the room burst on, blinding Pynthas and sending him onto his back, holding his hands over his eyes.

When he was able to see again, he gasped anew and nearly fainted—for there, hovering over his face like a metal balloon, was the High Leader's own visage, eyes burning bright with anger.

The High Leader pulled a thin-fingered front limb in a snapping motion over Pynthas's face; there, held delicately between two of the High Leader's metal nails, was the data card Pynthas had dropped.

"Get up," the High Leader said, moving away from the scrambling toady; on rising, Pynthas saw that the chamber, when bathed in light as it was now, was no different than any other chamber holding a Screen and no furniture; it had been the darkness, and the High Leader, which had made it fearsome.

The High Leader was pushing the data card into the Screen's receptacle.

Pynthas, deathly afraid for another reason now,

managed to take a tentative step forward and squeak out, "P-perhaps I sh-should explain . . . ?"

The High Leader turned with a withering glance, and Pynthas immediately froze in place.

"We'll watch it together," the High Leader said with annoyance. "I should tell you, Pynthas, that I'm amazed that I made you territorial governor of those infernal regions you abide so well—those . . ."

"Volcanic regions!" Pynthas said, with a trace of animation. "Arsia Mons, and Tholis Regis, and—"

"Yes, those dead volcanoes. Thank the sky there aren't any Martian citizens there you could harm. I should also point out that before you barged in on me I was enjoying a rather extraordinary Period of Darkness. In fact, I had been looking forward to it ever since my bargain was struck with Kamath Clan. It really was a most extraordinary piece of luck, you know. For the mere promise that the house of Clan remain united with the house of Kris, thereby fulfilling the silly woman's lifelong wish that her secular religion be accepted and legitimized on Mars—which it never will be, of course—she has sent Tabrel Kris back to me. In the process she has cut her own throat, of course, and probably that of her idiot son as well. At the same time, she has made sure that Wrath-Pei will cut short his acquisition raids on our outer colonies, and also guaranteed that the vermin will be on Titan when we strike."

The High Leader turned his glowering eyes on Pynthas Rei. "All of this I was enjoying with the utmost languorousness, Pynthas. I cannot describe to you how pleasant thoughts become even more pleasant when they are drawn out to exquisite length. It is one of the decidedly positive aspects of my . . . condition. And now, the message? I do hope it won't offend my still languorous mood."

"As I s-said, p-perhaps I should—"

"Screen, begin," the High Leader said, ignoring the toady's beseeching.

The Screen was filled with the ravaged, full-length picture of Senator Kris, suspended in his constraining upright field; the field's faint yellow light made the senator appear slightly jaundiced.

"Did the camera in the garret record this?"

"Yes, High Leader."

"Why is he smiling?" the High Leader asked.

"Because—" Pynthas began, but he was cut off not by the High Leader this time but by the senator, who began to speak.

"Prime Cor . . . nelian," Senator Kris rasped; his mouth was indeed smiling—a very unattractive sight, since his mouth had long since been voided of teeth, which had fallen out one by one over the years due to the intravenous diet he had been subjected to, which kept him just one side of malnutrition.

The senator tried to move; but the tightness of his constriction caused him a pain that he seemed to have long since come to terms with. His face resumed a more passive demeanor, but his lips moved, and he spoke:

"Prime . . . Corn . . . elian. I know that . . . you think . . . you have . . . won. But I . . . must tell you other . . . wise."

Exhausted by the effort, the senator seemed to drift

off to sleep; the High Leader, impatient, shouted at the Screen, "Move on!"

The Screen froze. "That is not a directive command."

The High Leader turned and shrieked at Pynthas, "Make it work!"

"Screen, resume," Pynthas whispered, cowering.

Instantly the senator began to speak again on the Screen.

"You . . . do not . . . under . . . stand my . . . daughter," he said. What the High Leader at first took to be a grin was actually a grimace. "For . . . even if you have . . . her body . . . she will . . . still resist you . . ."

The High Leader felt his rage rising to new high levels, and yet he was able to bark out a laugh. "I still have you—you old foo—"

The Screen image of the senator managed to cut the High Leader off, even though his voice was a bare breath. "If I . . . were to remain . . . alive, my . . . daughter would . . . do your . . . bidding. However . . ."

Now the senator did manage a smile, and now the withered, paper-skinned hand at his side flickered upward, ever so slightly; there was the tiniest glint of something metallic, and then the field around Senator Kris brightened to blindness and then collapsed, leaving the senator's blackened, charred body in a heap on the garret floor.

"*What—happened?*" the High Leader screeched, managing a sound that was something between a gasp and a howl of fury. He turned on Pynthas. "*What happened?*"

"He . . . t-t-terminated himself, High Lead—"

"*How? How could he do this?*" Prime Cornelian turned back to the Screen, staring with fascination at the senator's dead body, its burned head angled back as if on cue to face the camera, the skeletal look of its mouth looking not much different than the painful penultimate grin the senator had managed in life.

"He . . . had a . . ."

"*What?*"

". . . button, High Leader, a . . . metal button, which he . . . apparently hid in his palm when we put him in the . . . field. He . . . apparently was aware that it would . . . disrupt the phase and . . ."

Prime Cornelian said, "Do you mean to tell me that Senator Kris kept that *button* for three years, knowing that it could end his life at any time—end his pain—and yet he didn't use it until it was most useful for his *daughter*?"

"That would . . . appear to be the case, High Leader. It was actually easy for him to hold the button, since it was locked against his palm by the field—"

"That's not what I mean, you idiot!" Prime Cornelian drew even closer to the Screen, marveling at the senator's dead body. "Such . . . dedication. If only the Machine Master could manufacture *that* for me."

"Would you like me to . . . summon the Machine Master, High Leader?"

The High Leader turned, as if seeing Pynthas for the first time. "What? No, of course not, you dolt. Just . . . get out."

Pynthas, thankful for release, skittered backward toward the door.

"And turn out the lights on leaving."

"Yes, High Leader!" Pynthas fumbled for the switch, missing it twice before drawing the High Leader's attention.

"I said get out! I'll handle it myself!"

"Yes, High Leader!"

Fumbling still at the door, Pynthas Rei fell out into the hallway as the door opened unexpectedly behind him. As it began to close again, the lights were extinguished in the chamber, and the High Leader began to slip once more into a Period of Darkness. But now there was illumination in the room from the still-active Screen, before which Prime Cornelian had prostrated himself, as if hypnotized.

"A . . . maz . . . ing . . ." the High Leader said languidly, as the door closed tight in Pynthas Rei's face.

17

As an actor, Porto enjoyed immensely the Lost Lands.

Drama! The Lost Lands presented nothing if not drama: each moment was fraught with peril, the fight of mutant species that may have heaved into existence only the week or month before; the battle of twisted life that existed in a world where natural law had been turned upside down.

Action! The fights themselves—between four-eyed reptiles and three-eyed birds, for instance, provided plenty of that; there were minor skirmishes of a thousand varieties, and the constant, inevitable, age-old contest between hunter and prey. Since his departure from the rebel camp a week before, Porto had beheld tiny creatures with impossibly long limbs devour animals thrice their size by merely squeezing them to death; and then seen the same ten-meter-limb creatures bested by monsters half *their* size, who then proceeded to feast on both losers. Porto was less intrigued by the innards of these beasts; some seemed to ooze copper-colored sap in place of blood, and where there was blood it was too light in color to provide hope of normal human sustenance. Porto had, naturally, provided his own food for the trip.

Romance! Well, there wasn't much of that, except goggly-eyed things courting other goggly-eyed things, during which times Porto amused himself with the scenery.

Scenery! And what scenery it was! Worthy of any nightmare stage. At night in the Lost Lands thunder may or may not be accompanied by lightning or clouds; clouds themselves, never a fluffy white, often a rancid yellow or brown, may or may not produce acid rain. Lightning, in fact, found its way to the ground without benefit of storm—by benefit, in fact, of the skewed atmosphere, whose ionization layer had picked up enough charged electrons to produce lightning whenever it liked. The sky itself was a constant slate gray and produced the not-infrequent tornado funnel that tore through the blasted landscape, driving infertile blue-black soil into the air, along with the rusted roots of dead plants and mutant mixtures of plant and animal life: dun-leaved ferns with lionine features bulging from their stems, uprooted things walking with zombie gaits, daisies that screamed with the coming of each sickly dawn.

And the stage itself!

The stage!

Porto felt himself a man at home. Though he had had a few close calls, most of his days had been spent in happy contemplation at this thespian's paradise he found himself in. Not since his boyhood days, while acting for food in Cairo's slums, had he felt so free to improvise; his morning might be spent in happy soliloquy to a shivering (literally) oak tree; during an afternoon break from his northeastward trek, he might stop to serenade three leathery monsters in the process of devouring a chum, holding them in thrall with his juggling wizardry. Swamp globs, who thrived on acid rain, he discovered, were partial to jokes; so, too, were two-headed cranes biased in favor of the historical Shakespeare. Julius Caesar being Porto's specialty, he escaped more than one close call by rattling off the death scene: "Et tu, Brutus!"

And always, Porto was startled by something new. He discovered, for instance, that the reports of recent years had been true: that parts of the Lost Lands were not lost anymore. Here and there amid the supposed ruins were spots of new fecundity; where a few years earlier might have stood a stand of rotting elms, now these elms had found reason to thrive again, and flower green as ever their ancestors. Where a fetid swamp, filled with pestilence and drinkable death, had lain, now flowed a stream-fed pool of real water (a good thing, since at one point Porto's own water supply had been depleted during an unfortunate flight from ungrateful patrons who thought him food instead of food for thought). Here and there, a patch of real blue shone overhead—even if the shining be fleeting; and, once, a cloud of, yes, fluffy white made its appearance at undewy dawn— only to be devoured by acidic brothers later in the morning, naturally, but the appearance was duly noted, and applauded.

What did Porto make of it? Nothing, for that was not his job; but he made note nevertheless.

There were way stations: pseudo-principalities of human mutants and outcasts and, occasionally, other, smaller rebel camps. Through half of what had once been Africa, Porto was never without promise of aid for long, and often met with more deference than he was used to. One outer fiefdom feted him as if he were visiting royalty—though the dishes, which included among other delicacies six-toed monkey, were not to his liking, the attention was pleasing. Not a few dinners ended with impromptu performances by the traveling ambassador; his Cyrano, especially, was enjoyed on this occasion. Another camp provided a ride in a rickety contraption that mimicked the flight of an airplane; Porto enjoyed the shortening of the trip, if not the method.

And then, suddenly, he was on the edge of the World again. The sky cleared; the grass was green, the Lost Lands left behind. Now his situation became more official. There were officials to kowtow to, ceremonies to partake in. Here his acting served him more than well. When he left these borderline states behind, the goodwill he had engendered did nothing to endanger the recent alliances the rebels had made. For this, Porto was thankful.

And then, he was among the unfriendly.

It was an abrupt change; a borderline between governorships distinct perhaps on a map but not beneath Porto's feet. From friendly territory he passed one beautiful morning into unfriendly territory, and found himself surrounded by Imperial soldiers.

"Hello?" he said, seeking to keep the conversation light.

But these were serious fellows, the most serious of which held a bayoneted raser to his throat.

"You are?" the man said, with anything but friendliness.

"I am Porto, on an official mission to see Prime Minister Acron."

The bayonet flicked, and the man blinked.

"Keep him here," the soldier said, leaving Porto surrounded by merely five men with weapons, instead of six, while the soldier went off to check Porto's story.

He was back soon enough.

"Come with me," he ordered, and when Porto bowed in a theatrical fashion, he found the point of a bayonet in his derriere.

"Just follow," he was ordered, and thenceforth did as he was told.

There followed numerous trips in numerous forms of transport, mostly with blackened windows, at the end of which Porto found himself face-to-face with Acron himself, in the man's capacious office.

The man was drunk—a state which Porto wished himself to be in. He had already been roughed up, and knew that more of the same was on the way.

"So you were stupid enough to come, eh?" Acron said, poking at Porto with what looked like a sharpened metallic stick—but which proved to have a nasty electrical shock associated with its touch.

Porto flinched back, but Acron followed him closely with a parry, poking the weapon into the actor's belly.

"I was sent on a diplomatic mission—" Porto began in a dignified voice.

"Diplomatic?" Acron laughed, the sound breaking into a drunken cough. "Look at you! You don't look like a diplomat to me! From what I hear you're nothing but a second fiddle of an actor!"

Porto smiled, until the pig-eyed prime minister's stick once again found his midsection, imparting a nasty shock.

"I have been sent—" Porto said.

"You've been sent as a lamb to slaughter, you simpleton! Did you think I would truly negotiate with your band of cutthroats?"

"There was mention of a truce—"

"Ha! Bait! That's all it was—and look what it's caught!"

The prime minister jabbed the electric stick viciously at Porto, who nearly blacked out with its effect. When his eyes cleared, he was on the floor with fat Acron astride him, his bloodshot eyes full of malevolence.

"You're here, and you're mine," the prime minister growled. "I've murdered greater men than you with my bare hands. And once you tell me where your vermin compatriots are, I'll wipe them from the face of the Lost Lands as if they were toilet droppings."

In spite of his pain, Porto could not help his amusement. "What a colorful phrase—may I appropriate it?"

With another drunken growl the prime minister jabbed at Porto again, and this time Acron did not remove the stick for a long time, until Porto no longer felt the pain in consciousness.

He was tortured by experts. He had endured torture of a minor sort before, but these were sophisticated men. At first he had been able to act his way through the proceedings—but in the end, they had stripped him of all of his performance trappings until only the truth was left. And then they pulled the raw leavings of truth from him, leaving him weak, and drained, and feeling traitorous. When they finally left him alone he tried to hang himself, but was denied this exit and left weaponless and alone in his cell.

Acron did come to see him, after the fact. And though the fat prime minister was even drunker than when they had first met, he was smirking now, as he shouted through the bars of Porto's cell.

"You see, vermin? I told you this was how it would go! And now I will give you the privilege of living to see what your information will do to your friends! Now, when the High Leader drops his bombs on the Lost Lands, I will take you there afterward and make you lick the dead bones of your brothers!"

18

"Where *is* she?" Wrath-Pei demanded.

For the first time in a long time, something like a smile of pleasure found its way onto Kamath Clan's face. The Wrath-Pei she beheld on the Screen before her was one she had never before witnessed. The calm, chilling coldness was stripped away, revealing the animal within; and his eyes—if only she were close enough now to see into his seething eyes—close enough to claw them out with her bare fingers—

"She is somewhere you cannot get at her. On her way back to Mars."

"So it's true!" Wrath-Pei fumed. "You've actually smuggled her off Titan!"

"Yes, it's true," Queen Clan said. Even through her pain, she could not help showing her satisfaction.

"Are you *mad*? Do you know what you've done? You've given Cornelian every reason to attack without worry now! He'll destroy Titan!"

"He'll destroy you. And we've made a pact."

"A *pact*? You *are* mad! Treaties mean nothing to that creature! He'll annihilate all of us!"

"So be it. The House of Clan will survive, as will the Sect of Faran Clan. Even if I don't survive."

"You won't! And your religion means nothing to Cornelian either! He'll honor *nothing*!"

"Perhaps."

With a renewed measure of control, Wrath-Pei said, "Let me show you something, Queen Clan."

"As you wish."

Wrath-Pei held up a thin amber vial. "What if I told you I had succeeded in my . . . experiments?"

"I would say that it meant nothing to me now. Those times have passed; I no longer require what Quog provided. I have found . . . other things to dwell on."

"Other things? What other things could there be?" For a moment Wrath-Pei regained his old confidence and oily charm. "Not *religion*, I hope?"

Queen Clan returned silence for a moment before saying, "As I said, I have moved on to other things. Good-bye, Wrath-Pei."

"You fool!"

But the transmission went dead.

And, in his gyro chair, Wrath-Pei screamed and clutched at his snips, pulling them closed, and opened, and closed again.

On Io, Queen Kamath Clan turned from her own Screen and said, "Are you sure Wrath-Pei could not detect the relay?"

Jon-Ten, Minister of Faith, one of only two men on all of Titan whom the Queen knew she could trust implicitly, nodded his bald head. "I'm sure he thinks you are still on Titan."

"And he will proceed there?"

"With all due speed, no doubt."

"And you still believe General Pron-Kel can handle a Martian attack, if it comes?"

With a trace of smile, the priest said, "For a Martian, he is very much of Titan."

"Indeed."

Her gaze drifted from the secular priest for a moment; but when Jon-Ten cleared his throat politely, she gave him her attention once more.

"I have kept that much of my bargain with Prime Cornelian, at least," the Queen said. "How much time does this really give us, Jon-Ten?"

The priest puffed his cheeks full of air and let it out slowly while he pondered. "Perhaps a week; perhaps more. We both know how porous the royal ranks have become, my queen. I'm certain we escaped without detection. But sooner or later . . ." The man shrugged.

"Yes. Sooner or later . . ."

Again, Kamath Clan's gaze drifted away.

"My queen, are you . . . well?"

"I allowed myself to think for a moment of what Wrath-Pei claimed."

"That he had removed Quog's essence?"

"Yes."

"Unlikely. And even so . . ."

The queen's gaze slowly returned from its dreaming place and resumed its old air of resolve and aloofness; there was, however, a difference now, another kind of depth that softened the deep lines in

her face that withdrawal from Quog had etched, and
the pronounced stoop that her symptoms had forced
on her already unwieldy frame; she had always been
ugly, but now her ugliness had marked itself in new
ways—she had, with an irony that she did not comprehend, attained some of Quog's own deformities
concurrent with his withdrawal from her body.

"And the girl?" Queen Clan asked simply.

"She continues to sleep, I wager."

"My own potions are still powerful. And useful."

"It is only a shame that in Jamal's case . . ."

Again the queen's gaze slipped elsewhere. "For his
sake only, I would think further on Wrath-Pei's
claim."

"My queen!" Jon-Ten said, alarmed.

"But that would be foolish. So we are where we are."

"Yes, my queen."

"Prepare the ceremony, then."

"It will take a day, at least."

"Proceed, then," Kamath Clan ordered.

The Cleansing Ritual was as old as the philosophy
of Moral Guidance itself. Faran Clan had, it was told,
come up with the ceremony after the most rigorous
of his self-inflicted tests. It was said with some certainty that Moral Guidance was born only after Faran
Clan had absorbed every teaching of every religion
and philosophy, from the ancients to his own time,
digested and distilled them all down to their essence.
At the time, during the Religious Wars in the middle
of the twenty-second century, he was being held in
an Earth prison for sedition and other crimes, and it

was during this period of the famous Ninety-four Days, when he went, it was claimed, with neither water nor food to sustain him—only these teachings of morality handed down from the dawn of man— that the teachings of Moral Guidance were fully formulated.

And it was Faran Clan's son, Pen Clan, who led his followers to newly settled Titan, where the secular religion flourished after persecution on Earth and failure on Mars.

But Io—sulfurous, yellow, ravaged, volcanic, odorous Io—had always been the movement's mecca from the very beginning.

It was the cleansing musk of sulfur that had become central to the philosophy of Moral Guidance from the very beginning. It was sulfur, pure, yellow, primeval, elemental, whose properties Faran Clan and his followers found most conducive to their thoughts and symbolic of their thought.

"*Sulfur*," Faran Clan had written, during his second stay in prison during 2157, when his treatise was composed, "*denotes both heaven and earth. It is the most elemental of elements, distinctive, pleasant to the touch, yet malevolent when misused. It is the nature of man distilled to nonorganic matter. It is man itself, in symbol.*"

And Moral Guidance put great store in ceremony and symbol, for Faran Clan taught that balance between soul and body could only be attained within by attaining it without. Balance outside the flesh was essential, and desirable, for the attainment of peace, which was Moral Guidance's goal.

And thus the great Temple of Faran Clan on Titan, and the others elsewhere.

And the ceremonies held within.

The temple on Io was, secretly, even larger than that on Titan. During the early days on Titan, when the movement's success was in no way certain on the newly colonized moon, Pen Clan, with the help of certain wealthy interests, had secretly undertaken a project on Io in case the Titanian experiment was a failure. After Titan, otherwise, there would be nowhere to go; Pluto was in the early stages of terraforming and was slated only for partial taming—and even then, besides the building of a single city to exploit mining and research, the planet would be used as nothing more than a prison—something the followers of Moral Guidance were well acquainted with and sought at all risks to avoid in the future. That left undeveloped territory; specifically, to the followers of Moral Guidance, it left Io.

Io was already much in their province; as a provider of sulfur so dear to their ceremonies, the movement had naturally been involved in this moon of Jupiter's limited development. Only that development had been more extensive than the ore commerce it hid. While sulfur was being dug from beneath the surface of Io, other construction was being done within also. Caverns as spectacular as any found naturally or otherwise on the Five Worlds were excavated, and then, within these underground grottos of yellow-gold, were built secret monuments to Moral Guidance.

The most spectacular was the Temple of Io itself.

*   *   *

And this, then, was where Kamath Clan went for the Cleansing Ritual.

Already underground, she preferred to walk rather than take the open transport provided for such a trip. As had her walks through the Ruz Balib section on Titan, these walks afforded her the time she needed to contemplate what needed contemplation. There was much, now, as there had been much for some time, such as her worries over Titan, which she had unwillingly left behind; though it might soon fall into Martian hands, that fate was preferable to Wrath-Pei's continued rule. And the Martians, she was convinced, could be dealt with, while Wrath-Pei could not. After all, she still had the girl, Tabrel Kris, to bargain with, and she was convinced that Prime Cornelian would, if he chose to overlook her present treachery as a strategic move, allow her to continue to rule Titan (albeit as a Martian protectorate) in trade for her return of Princess Kris. She had little illusion about Cornelian's promise of reconciliation between Mars and Titan on the question of the unification of the Houses of Kris and Clan. Though the Martian despot might eschew his promise of public acknowledgment, the act was already a fait accompli; while Tabrel Kris remained married to Jamal, the two houses were already united, whether by public declaration or not. And since Queen Clan was convinced that the girl would be kept alive by Cornelian, it made no difference that the union was not a physical one. It had not been to this point, anyway—so what

if a few million miles distance was added to the bride
and groom's separation?

Jamal . . .

Here, then, was her great worry. As the queen
made her shuffling way through the faintly sulfur-
scented tunnel, whose faint illumination sent strange
lemon shadows against the walls, she thought on her
only son. He was a problem. Shuffling past his room,
she heard him moaning within. Slated to one day
rule Titan (in whatever capacity that rule would as-
sume, as Martian protectorate or otherwise) but, even
more importantly, set to oversee, as Faran Clan's direct descendant, the reaches of Moral Guidance itself,
Jamal was, at the moment, incapable of either. As she
thought of what he had become . . .

A spasm overtook the queen; she stopped, putting
her hands on the soft yellow rock walls of the tunnel
for support until it passed. She doubted these inter-
mittent pains would ever cease completely; while the
current pain persisted, her mind was blank, and then
she gradually returned to herself.

Poor Jamal . . .

Once again, thoughts of her son entered her mind.
While Quog's essence had eventually given the
queen up, and Tabrel (to the point where she needed
other of Kamath's potions to be kept under control),
it had, in the case of Jamal, done something quite
different.

Would he ever rule?

In either capacity?

Shuffling on, Kamath Clan turned her mind to different things—to, specifically, the ceremony awaiting

her in the temple, whose intricately carved portal at the end of the tunnel she now approached.

"Behold within these walls the mind and soul of Clan!"

The words, spoken by Jon-Ten, echoed portentously in the empty temple. Above the priest's place at the altar, the temple's ceiling fled upward, lost in misty heights of sulfurous incense. The temple's apex actually protruded from Io's surface above, letting in a glint of natural light; but it was well hidden and had never been detected.

With the help of artificial lighting, the temple's immensity became immediately evident. It dwarfed its sister structure on Titan; and though the workmanship on Titan's structure had been superb, the best materials had been saved for Io's secret shrine. The walls, of precious forest wood, were carved with details from Faran Clan's writings depicting the aeons of man's struggle with his own mind, and the search for his own soul. Veritably, the history Faran Clan had absorbed and distilled was here for all to see.

"Enter, and allow the Cleansing Ritual to begin!"

Kamath Clan stepped completely into the temple, letting the tunnel's portal close with an echoing clang behind her. The odor of sulfur was nearly overpowering, but Kamath Clan drank it in.

As the queen approached the altar, Jon-Ten drew back from the bath of roiling yellow; his bright yellow robes issued the steam they had absorbed, making him appear for a moment afire.

Queen Clan drew open her own yellow robe, preparing to step into the bath—

There came a piercing scream, which stayed Kamath Clan's foot even as it hovered over the steaming liquid sulfur.

A second piercing scream sounded—like death itself.

"*Jamal*," Queen Clan breathed.

She hurried from the temple, the priest following.

As she opened the portal door into the tunnel, she was met by four black-leather-clad figures, wearing odd-shaped boots and gloves to outline their various missing limbs.

Two of the soldiers took an immediate hold on Queen Clan, while the other two fired rasers simultaneously at the priest, Jon-Ten, who had stopped, startled, in the open portal and then turned to run. He was cut down with both shots in the back and fell dead to the ground.

A third piercing scream came from Jamal's room down the tunnel.

"My son!"

Without a word, the black-clad soldiers began to drag the queen toward Jamal's room; when they arrived, they stopped outside.

A fourth scream, horrible to Kamath Clan's ears, issued from within; then the door was opened, and Wrath-Pei's gyro chair, guided by the boy Lawrence from behind, glided from the room and stopped before the queen. Within, Kamath's view was blocked by more black-clad soldiers.

The tunnel's sulfurous odor was subsumed by a

sweet coppery smell. Wrath-Pei lovingly wiped something viscous and red from the tip of his shears and sheathed them.

He looked at Queen Clan and smiled.

"Happy to see me?" he said.

19

Benel Kran called him the Ghost.

Benel felt like something of a ghost himself. Ever since the war, which had taught him survival skills he had never dreamed of needing, he had avoided human contact. In the beginning, with Martian Marines rounding up every child and plasma soldiers killing every adult, Benel Kran had found himself some very interesting hiding places. The most interesting, and uncomfortable, had been the hollow inside of a feeder tube support column; once inside, Benel had quickly deduced that he was both safe from capture and probably dead anyway, since the squared opening of the tube was now fifty feet above his head and he, at the bottom, had no way to climb out.

But fate, in the form of luck, had helped him out, as the Martians, not content with their plunder of the feeder tube itself, decided to take its support columns also; after a little jostling, followed by a quick change of direction as the tube was craned from vertical to horizontal, he found himself in the open, at night, under a glorious mantle of stars in a now-empty work area. The next day he watched what had been his prison for five days hauled away atop a massive ground shuttle; watched, through his right eye only, since the cheap corneal implants he had foolishly favored over eyeball replacement had favored him with the left one peeling away and lost, from the safety of a smaller and more convenient hiding place, through the tiny window of a locked (he had jammed the lock himself) construction toilet.

The first six months after the war's quick end had gone this way, with Benel always in hiding, often close to capture, but managing to retain his freedom. *Not bad for a physicist,* he had thought.

And then, gradually, the planet had become quiet.

He watched the Martian Marines pull out from an empty house in Frolich City; out the kitchen window a breeze was moving a child's swing on its creaking chain; and, through the space between the chains, and through his right eye, Benel watched the sleek orange Martian Marine shuttles take off, one by one down a row, as if peeling away. Inside those rockets were the last of Venus's children and loot. In a few moments they were gone, along with their hissing stream of rocket fire.

Suddenly Benel felt alone, sitting there on a stool munching from a sealed can of peanuts he had found (food had never been a problem from the beginning: the Martians had stripped off anything they favored, but there were many foodstuffs the Martians did not favor, which had left Benel with plenty to eat from a rather restricted menu: dried cereals, nuts, anything generally dry; the Martians greatly prized Venus's store of vegetables and especially canned fruits, which Benel had come to sorely miss) and watching the last vapors of the Martian rockets dissipate into the powder-blue sky. But his loneliness was short-lived, as a plasma soldier appeared in the backyard, sending Benel scrambling for the house's attic, a trail of dropped peanuts behind him.

Which would have sealed his fate, had a Marine been hunting him; but as it was, his perpetual luck held and the plasma soldier, after a cursory examination of the house, went the way he had come.

And then, soon after, the light soldiers were gone, also.

Their leaving was much more abrupt, and spectacular. Benel, having become a nocturnal scrounger, was poking through a trash heap of tools the Martians had left in the middle of a public street when a monstrous humming sound commenced. When Benel looked around, it seemed the night sky was filled with bright shafts of light bursting from the ground to the sky. Only after the fact did Benel realize that what he had witnessed was the plasma soldiers being dematerialized, literally sucked back up to their orbital transmitters.

They were gone—just like that.

"Amazing," Benel said, out loud, the first words he had uttered in more than half a year.

He spent the next months being careful, because *someone* was still bound to be around. And he was not wrong. There were still plasma soldiers to be found, but they were easy to avoid, since their only function seemed to be to guard Venus's remaining feeder tube stations. Food storehouses and equipment dumps were out of their range of orders (they had absolutely no volition of their own), and so Benel was free to raid them as he wished.

The Martian Marine presence was, however, ended; and though a few Martian technicians still puttered around here and there, they were even easier to avoid than the plasma soldiers. Being engineers, they were generally loud and clumsy, and disliked to be inconvenienced.

They, too, eventually left, after denuding the planet of whatever they felt might be valuable.

Which left (if one didn't count the robotlike plasma soldiers) only Benel.

And the Ghost.

Benel stumbled upon the Ghost on what he later calculated to be the first anniversary of the One-Day War. The physicist had spent the preceding months establishing a laboratory of sorts in what had once been Frolich City's recreation center. Game tables, he found, made excellent lab benches, and the colorful gaming room had soon been converted into something else, its billiard tables overflowing with electrical equipment, its dart board supporting the thick line of an antenna cable, the smooth long line of its bar sporting beakers and electronic circuit boards where once drinks and pretzel bowls had ruled. The huge Screen, which covered one wall to the left of the bar, had once shown sporting events from Venus and the other Four Worlds; now it showed, alternately, the wavy frequency lines of test equipment and the crystal-clear picture from the security cameras Benel had mounted on the recreation center's roof and jerry-built into the system.

That was how Benel first saw the Ghost.

On what he later realized was the war's anniversary, Benel was absorbed, as he had been all day, and all month, and all year, in miniaturization problems. For Benel, who was not an engineer, it was not the basic problems that were bothersome, but the practical application of them. This, of course, had been his main concern during and after the war. It was something Cast-Prin, a fellow physicist, would have helped him with in a second—but Cast-Prin, unfortunately, had not made it through the war. And now that Benel Kran had every single theoretical problem solved in his project—he had, in effect, solved, a day too late, the problem of how to neutralize the plasma soldiers—he had no way to test it out. The mess of cables, circuitry, and other paraphernalia could only be tested if, incongruously, a plasma soldier walked in front of it. Which wasn't about to happen, since Benel had chosen a place where plasma soldiers would not bother to come.

Benel was bent over a particularly nasty nest of wiring, trying to squeeze it into a bulky, unattractive chromium box (how did those engineers manage to make everything look so elegant?) when the chiming alarm on the security camera system went off and the Screen broadened into a view of the outside perimeter.

A lone figure was making its way past the recreation center, with no apparent interest in the center, or anything else, for that matter.

"Screen, zoom," Benel ordered—but by the time the Screen obliged, the figure had rounded a corner and was lost to the camera's sight.

Benel hurried from the lab to the street and cautiously looked out.

But the streets were as empty as they had been before the appearance of the mysterious figure.

Thinking himself prone to hallucination, Benel returned to the lab and had the Screen review the pictures of the intruder; sure enough, he had been real, though Benel could not make out his features and he seemed vague in other ways—like a man not entirely in control of his own faculties.

"Wonderful, a crazy man," Benel mumbled, returning to his work and forgetting for a moment the vision. As long as he didn't bother Benel, the crazy man could do whatever he wanted. The brief thought that the crazy man might bring the attention of the plasma soldiers to Benel's laboratory gave Benel pause, but he dismissed the threat with a vow to set up his weapon facing the front entrance, just in case. Then, if a visit from the light soldiers should occur, he could, at the very worst, test the machine as they stormed in.

Crazy man . . .

Ghost . . .

Maybe I'll never see him again. . . .

But the Ghost did appear again, the next day, under similar circumstances, though this time in the midst of a rain shower. The streets of Frolich City were being pounded with rain, and above the sound of it on the thin resin roof of the recreation center

Benel did not at first hear the chime of the alarm
system. By the time he did look up at the Screen, the
Ghost was already disappearing, hatless and umbrel-
laless, around the same corner that had hid him the
day before; and, once again, as Benel reached the
street there was no sign of him anywhere.

He may be a ghost, Benel thought, *but I'll find out
what he's up to.*

And so, the next day, under bright sunshine, Benel
climbed early up onto the roof and, pushing puddles
from yesterday's storm aside with his boots, rea-
ligned one of the security cameras to give a wider
sweep.

The Ghost didn't appear that day or the next, leading Benel to think that perhaps he was gone for good,
or captured, or dead—

But the following day the security chime went off,
and Benel gave his full attention to the Screen.

"Zoom, and follow," Benel ordered, and the Screen
obeyed. Benel could almost feel the roof camera
swiveling to follow the Ghost—but still he could not
get a good look. The man's face was averted, hidden
in shadow. He walked like a person in a dream, unheedful of his surroundings, hands at his sides. His
tunic looked as if he had worn it for days.

In the labyrinthine streets surrounding the recreation center, Benel followed him until he was finally
lost in the distance. Benel was amazed to see that he
was heading for Frolich City's feeder station, but the
camera's limited range could not overcome distance,
and the Ghost was soon, once again, lost from sight.

"We'll see about this," Benel said.

And so began a six-month campaign to track the Ghost to his lair. Two months for Benel to find, and install, a superior surveillance system, salvaged from Martian equipment partially damaged by raser fire; Benel had to design circuitry to replace what was blown out in the Martian rig; it took two weeks alone to find a single Venusian part that did what an inefficient Martian one, with twenty times the components, had done. In the end, though, Benel Kran had his camera and had it mounted so that it could cover the landscape to the horizon. It could almost reach into space, so sensitive were its optics.

But then the Ghost didn't come.

Four more months passed, during which time Benel struggled with his miniaturization problems. He still longed for a plasma soldier to test the rig, as bulky and unwieldy as it was. Eventually, the Ghost slipped from Benel's mind. Occasionally the security system, overly sensitive, was set off by a high-flying bird and, once, by a groundhog appearing in the mouth of its burrow a half mile away. The system became an annoyance, and Benel determined to dismantle it.

And then the Ghost returned.

A darkening, gray, cloudy day this time, with rain promised for later. Benel was not even in the lab, but had given himself a day off, to be spent trying to come up with something new to eat. He was in the recreation center's supply closet, going over cartons and cans of dried foods, trying to figure out a way of spicing up their various combinations, when the chime of the security system went off out in the lab.

"The groundhog returns!" Benel said to himself; but the chime was insistent.

Sighing, Benel went to the lab.

And there, on the Screen, was the Ghost.

Benel stared for a moment, openmouthed, not so much at the appearance of the Ghost but at the sensitivity and excellence of the equipment Benel had installed. He was nearly looking into the Ghost's tunic pockets, so good was the camera's resolution. And yet, the figure's features were still a blur. Benel squinted his one good eye at the Screen, but the best he could make out was a face oddly blackened and a scruffy beard. The man's tunic was positively filthy; Benel was sure that he had not looked this unkempt before. His hands were palsied, and he walked oddly, as if sure where he was going and yet still tentative.

"Zoom on face," Benel ordered, and the camera tried, but the Ghost had already turned away from the recreation building and was shuffling toward the edge of the city.

"Follow," Benel commanded.

And the camera did so, splendidly, keeping the Ghost's back centered in the picture and anticipating his reappearance when he was blocked from view by an occasional building.

At the edge of Frolich City the Ghost did not stop; he was heading for the feeder station.

"Amazing," Benel said.

And even more amazing: when he reached the outskirts of the station, where plasma soldiers could plainly be seen on station, their thin yellow bodies made of light standing like sentries, the Ghost was able to continue unimpeded into the feeder station itself; the camera followed the Ghost's slow progress up catwalks and into maintenance buildings, passing sentries without acknowledgment or challenge—as if the Ghost really were a ghost.

After some time—hours may have passed, but Benel was so absorbed in this strange drama that he paid no heed to time—the Ghost left the feeder station and reentered Frolich City, taking a different route than he had formerly, which would give him wide berth past Benel's lab.

Benel's first impulse was, suitably armed, to confront the Ghost on his return trip; the street the Ghost was walking was a wide thoroughfare only a few blocks away, and Benel could be there in ambush in plenty of time; he had even put this plan into effect and was outside the lab, bearing a large pipe, when a sudden thought struck him.

Dropping the pipe, Benel ran back to face the Screen once more: there was the Ghost, face partly averted, shambling up Frolich City's main street, named Frolich Avenue; the wide boulevard looked dusty and empty, a few abandoned vehicles, some on their sides, pushed up against the curb: a suitably empty street for an empty world. The Ghost looked, indeed, like the last man on Venus: alone, wandering, yet purposeful. Benel thought he, too, might look this way to someone else.

Benel followed the Ghost's progress through and then out of Frolich City. The afternoon wore on, grayer and darker yet devoid of rain, as clouds built over distant Sacajawea Patera's cone, toward which the Ghost seemed inevitably drawn.

"Screen, zoom," Benel ordered, and the surveillance camera did its best, as the Ghost's figure diminished, but not before Benel was sure he saw it board the lift at the volcano's base, taking it up to the Piton, the facility set like a spike into the peak's breast, a hundred yards from its summit.

"Zoom, Screen!"

"Camera is at peak zoom factor," the Screen reported dispassionately.

But the camera did follow up the side of Sacajawea Patera, and then, as it focused on the darkened Piton, Benel was rewarded with the lights flaring on within the structure, which was bordered on all sides by glass; like a wife seeking the return of her wandering husband, the Ghost had lit a lamp in the window.

"Screen off," Benel said—which was just as well, since it had started to rain in the near distance between the volcano and Frolich City, making the picture awash and indistinct.

But the lamp was lit.

And Benel knew he was the wandering husband, who would make the trip to that wayward lamp.

Having retrieved his lead pipe and packed food for a good day's trip, Benel set out for Sacajawea the next morning, before the sun rose.

It had rained for only a few hours, and late in the night a cold front had moved the clouds away and dried the air and sky.

Earth was up, blue and bright, with the tiny chip

of its Moon riding its waist. The air was refreshingly
chilled. Benel knew he would be unmolested on the
trip; before leaving, he had, just to make sure,
checked the feeder station, comforting himself with
the fact that all of its light soldiers stood unmoving
at their posts, yellow smudges against the darkness.
There might be animals to contend with, a rogue dog
or mountain cat come down from the Patera looking
for food; but most of these were not desperate or
large enough to attack a man, since there was still
plenty of game and food around for even a bad
hunter.

Benel had thought briefly of lugging his light soldier degenerator with him, perhaps pulled behind on
a cart; there might, after all, be plasma soldiers at the
Piton—but had dismissed the idea as foolish. He had,
however, taken the precaution of dismantling the
various components and hiding them in separate
places around the lab. A little caution was worth
much deflected pain.

By starlight, he had no trouble making his way
from the city. He cut over to Frolich Avenue, as the
Ghost had, and was soon in the scrubby area between the city and the volcano.

It occurred to him that he had never dared visit
the Piton before—and it occurred to him now that
even if the Ghost wasn't there, or proved to be a real
ghost and thus invisible, the trip would be worth it
for the salvage possibilities alone.

Thus buoyed, he made progress faster than he supposed he would, and, as dawn began to break, shed-
ding night's stars and the blue coin of Earth and its

diamond moon, Benel Kran found himself at the foot of Sacajawea Patera, scouting for plasma soldiers that did not exist.

The lift tube was not in good shape; it had been damaged, no doubt, in the One-Day War, and gave an ominous repeated creak on descending, which caused Benel to hide in the shadows until it stopped and opened, empty.

He climbed in, helping the door closed when it seemed incapable of performing the task itself, and spoke into the lift's activator, "Rise."

With a reversed tone, the former creak returned, repeated every few seconds as the lift lurched upward.

At one point there was a horizontal rather than vertical lurch, which greatly alarmed Benel; through the lift's clear glass he saw that a portion of the track had been blasted away, burned black around the edges—but after a moment of strain the lift continued upward and gained its destination.

Benel had spent very little of the trip enjoying the view of the valley he had just traveled, now bathed in rose dawn that led back to Frolich City and, to its right, reflecting new light on its glinting surface, Lake Clotho Tessera, and the stillborn community on its shores, Lakshmi Planum; most of his attention, rather, had been spent on the dangerous cage he rode.

But now that the lift had reached the Piton, Benel turned full attention away from machinery and landscape and waited for the doors to open.

They did not, groaning against their mechanisms;

and, try as he might, Benel, once again giving his full attention to machinery, could not get them to open.

Giving up for a moment in frustration, Benel was startled to hear a soft voice from the other side of the door:

"You must kick it at the bottom."

Benel did as he was told, gripping his lead pipe all the tighter as the doors suddenly sprung open.

The room before him looked empty—filled with dawn's new light, which washed up through the quartz-windowed floor and streamed into the other windows—a room of light.

No ghost . . .

Yes—there he was:

The Ghost was there at the farthest jutting of the Piton; there was so much new light in the room that it refracted around the Ghost, making him nearly invisible.

"I've been waiting for you," the Ghost said quietly, hands behind its back; it did not turn, but seemed to be staring at the rising Sun before it.

"Please," the Ghost said quietly,' "come stand beside me and talk."

Still clutching the pipe, Benel made his way cautiously through the room, negotiating the wreckage within—knocked-over tables, piles of blueprints ripped in half, the wreckage of numerous meticulously built models, now dashed and crushed and pushed into corners.

Still not at ease, Benel waited for something to jump out at him from behind an overturned table, perhaps; there were, after all, places for light soldiers, or other ghosts, to hide.

"You needn't be afraid," the Ghost said, sensing his caution. "We're alone here." There was eerie calm in the Ghost's voice, which made Benel even more cautious.

The Ghost held out a hand, still not turning.

"Please."

Benel stepped up beside the Ghost, who put a soft hand on him, testing his own corporeality, perhaps.

"Yes, you've come," the Ghost said, with something like peaceful relief.

Even through the ravaged features, Benel knew who the Ghost was now: Carter Frolich himself. Even behind the dirt, and crusted blood, and through the growth of filthy beard, and madness, Benel recognized Venus's founder.

Frolich smiled, his soft hand still on Benel, the trembling fingers barely touching, afraid to proceed or let go, perhaps. His mouth smiled slightly, his sightless, empty, blood-dried eye sockets continuing to stare at the rising magnificent Sun, which hurt Benel's eyes, making him avert his gaze.

"Yes, you've come," Carter Frolich said. "I read *King Lear*, you know, and knew that you would visit if I did that. Thank you for coming," Frolich continued, and Benel was amazed to see a tear forming in the corner of one of the man's ruined eyes. "Venus is safe," Frolich continued. "I just wanted to tell you that myself. Venus is safe. After all, that's all I ever wanted. And I wanted to say I'm sorry."

Benel flinched as Carter Frolich grabbed him suddenly by both arms, bringing his crying face close to Benel's own.

"I'm sorry, Targon!" Frolich pleaded, and Benel, caught in the man's madness, could do nothing but listen. *"I'm sorry, Targon Ramir!"*

20

As easily as they had boarded Wrath-Pei's ship, they disembarked it.

Dalin Shar and Shatz Abel found themselves, on Titan, no closer to their destination or to their other goals. During their weeks on Wrath-Pei's vessel they had never come close to facing Wrath-Pei himself; had never, despite numerous attempts, been able to even *locate* Wrath-Pei. His ship had been a labyrinth of both physical and hierarchical design; no one seemed to know where Wrath-Pei was at any time, and the layers of command were both shifting and amorphous. The closest they had come to Wrath-Pei was a brief encounter with Wrath-Pei's protégé Lawrence, who, his head wrapped as always in his communications helmet, had passed by their work-station once—but by the time they gave pursuit, Lawrence had hobbled away, lost in a matrix of corridors.

"Well, we learned little enough," Shatz Abel said, making his way with Dalin and a hundred other black-clad workers into Titan's streets on leave. A handful of soldiers passed them by, slapping either Shatz

Abel or Dalin or both on the back and wishing them well.

"See you in two days, boys! Enjoy your leave. It'll be the last till after the war!"

Feigning heartiness, Shatz Abel called after them with greetings, mumbling under his breath after they had gone that he would rather have wrung their necks.

"Learned little enough?" Dalin said, when they were at last alone. "How can you say that? We know everything there is to know about bilge pumps, and waste backups, and blow tubes." With a disgusted sound he tore off his gloves and threw them into the nearest waste bin. Shatz Abel followed suit.

"Let's find some real clothes, then, lad," the pirate said.

"And some real food," Dalin said. Making a face, he continued, "I never was completely sure that what we were eating wasn't . . . human." He rubbed at the clipped area around his eyes. "Given Wrath-Pei's predilections and all."

Shatz Abel nodded, "Nor I," he said.

They stopped to watch, behind a phalanx of troops, the disembarking of Queen Kamath Clan and, behind her, in a cagelike box born by four men, her raving son, who clutched at the bars of his prison, pulling his legless torso forward and screaming, "I am King! War is upon you! Prepare to die!"

Howling in pain that turned to laughter, the prince and his haggard-looking mother were escorted away, under Titan's lights which gave an illusion of day.

"Will Wrath-Pei keep them alive?" Dalin asked soberly.

Shatz Abel nodded. "He'll do that, and worse. Especially with war coming."

Dalin said, "I wish Tabrel were here on Titan."

Again the pirate nodded. "At least it would give us a reason to be on this mudball. Instead of a reason to leave."

The two men searched for a apparel shop, the sooner to shed themselves of the uniforms they wore.

"I will ask you again, Queen Klan: where is Tabrel Kris?"

Back in the queen's own lodgings, Wrath-Pei thought that Kamath Clan might feel more inclined to speak, but this was not so. He knew Jamal could no longer be used as a bargaining chip; for his part, he felt almost angry at himself for not waiting. But when he had seen the boy, lying whole there as he had been on Io, untouched, *whole*, something had overtaken him. He had envisioned the moment for so long that when it finally came, he could not help himself. He had given himself a present.

The queen now knew that what Wrath-Pei had begun he would never stop—and therefore it was useless to try to fool her by promising to leave Jamal alone.

Oh, well: that did not matter. It may have worked quicker. But he had another means of obtaining what he wanted.

Wrath-Pei leaned forward in his gyro chair; the chair's gimbals whirred and adjusted, and, behind the chair, Lawrence's faceplate brightened briefly with data flowing across its inside surface.

"Queen Clan," Wrath-Pei said in a conspiratorial whisper, "I was not, ah, shall we say, *lying* regarding the success of my experiments on our friend Quog."

The queen's expression did not change.

"What would you say," Wrath-Pei continued, drawing from a pocket next to his shears on the chair's side a thin long silver tube, "if I were to tell you that I had, indeed, been able to ... *simulate* Quog's essence?"

Now there was a flicker of interest; the queen's glance darted for a moment to the silver receptacle.

"Even were that true," Queen Clan said, her voice flat, "it would make no difference. I have reached a plain of acceptance—"

"I know, I know," Wrath-Pei said impatiently. "Spare me the religious claptrap about how you no longer require what I have. The truth is, you *were* addicted"—He motioned to two leather-clad soldiers, who flanked the queen and now put their hands on her, to force compliance as Wrath-Pei opened the thin flask and brought the contents close to Kamath Clan's resisting lips—"and will soon be addicted again."

With a look of distaste, Wrath-Pei handed the silver tube to a third soldier for administration; he watched for a moment the queen's failed resistance and then motioned for his chair to be turned away.

"Let me know when she is fully under the influence," Wrath-Pei said, to which the soldiers immediately assented. "She will then tell us where the girl is. Until then I will be ... occupied."

Wrath-Pei's hand fell to the holster on the side of

his chair; already his thoughts had turned to the queen's son.

In new clothes that made them comfortable but noticeable, Dalin and Shatz Abel made their way to the Ruz Balib section, only to find that most of the pirate's old hangouts had been either closed or recently converted to military installations. All of Titan was on alert; and those citizens or soldiers they passed in the street had a grave, determined look on their faces. Even in the Ruz Balib section, where commerce had always existed side by side with government, there was a new seriousness that worried Shatz Abel.

"This isn't the Titan I remember!" the pirate marveled. "This used to be a place where you could get something done right on the table! Face-to-face! Now all the businessmen are gone! These people all look like . . . warmongers!"

"I was always told of the fierceness of the Titanians," Dalin said. "From the look of these people, I can believe it."

There were in the street, keeping to the shadows, having come up empty after five attempts to find Shatz Abel's old cronies. The latest haunt, which had been a nightclub, was now a munitions factory; people passed them with grim faces, hurrying to get where they were going.

"It looks like war *is* imminent, doesn't it?" Dalin ruminated.

Shatz Abel concurred. "And we'd better get off Titan before it happens, Sire."

*   *   *

Inevitably, they ended up back where they had
begun, by the shuttle port. Only now, dressed as they
were, they had to avoid the same black-clad soldiers
they had been laughing and commiserating with not
hours before.

There was a commotion at the farthest dock; before
even Shatz Abel could react, Dalin Shar grinned
widely and said, "I may have an answer to our
problems!"

There, arguing outside the beat-up wreck of their
freighter, were old acquaintances of Dalin's: Ralf and
Enry, pirates who had picked him up when the
freight container the king was in was about to be
dashed to bits; they had taught him the pirating
trade—and also had turned him over to Wrath-Pei.

The two pirates were arguing with a uniformed
dock official; beside them on the tarmac was a pile
of cases, one of which was broken open.

"I tell you, it's Titanian wine!" Enry protested, as
the soldier tilted a chrome bottle up and tasted its
contents, making a face. "Bought it ourselves, we did,
right here on Titan!"

"Ri'!" Ralf said, backing up his partner. He leaned
close to the soldier and said in a half whisper, "An'
a case of it is yours, mate, if you'll just le' us be on
our way. . . ."

Ralf winked, squeezing the soldier's arm in a
friendly way.

The soldier spat out the wine and made a face.
"This is swill! I'll throw the two of you in prison—"

"There, there, now," Ralf said, patting the soldier's

hand with his own, which held a wad of currency. "If you'll jus' take this . . . *gift*, there need be no trouble and you can give us our launch clearance data card—"

"A bribe!" the soldier sputtered, letting the bills flutter to the ground. "I'll have you in irons!"

"What's the trouble?" Shatz Abel said, grinning from ear to ear at the soldier, while Dalin smiled at Enry and Ralf, who stood dumbfounded.

"It's—" Enry sputtered.

"That it is!" Ralf said in wonder, staring at Dalin. "Minus 'is eyelids, of course."

"What is this nonsense?" the official shouted—but Shatz Abel had already advanced on him, still grinning.

In a moment the dock official, unconscious, was being dragged by Shatz Abel into a dark recess behind a nearby gantry, while Dalin helped Enry and Ralf restock their wine into the open hold of the ship and follow it inside.

"Jus' li' ol' times, eh, Your Majesty?" Enry said, beaming.

"Ri'!" his companion chimed in. "Jus' li' ol' times!"

In another moment Shatz Abel returned, bearing a launch clearance data card, and climbed whistling into the ship's hold after the others; after a few preliminaries, the creaking freighter took off, and was soon clear of Titan.

"Earth!" Enry said, shaking his head. "Not likely, mate. We'll be lucky if we gets t' Mars with the load we have." He turned from the ship's front view to grin apologetically up at Shatz Abel.

The big pirate took the entire front of the man's tunic in his fist; in his other hand he held Ralf in a similar manner.

"O' course, we could change our plans, couldn't we, Enry?" Ralf said. "I mean this being the great Shatz Abel and all?"

Enry nodded meekly. "I suppose we could a' that."

"You'll do it," Shatz Abel said sternly, nodding in Dalin's direction, "for him."

"Ri'!" Ralf said. "Was on my mind all along, it was!"

"For king and country, an' all tha'!" Enry said.

Shatz Abel said, looking from one to the other, "Do you know how many times I had to hear the story about how you two gave Dalin over to Wrath-Pei? Do you know how sick I became of hearing that tale?"

Meekly, the two pirates looked at Dalin.

"We're truly sorry, we are, Sire," Enry said meekly.

"Truly sorry. We was victims of circumstance, we was."

"That's ri'!" Enry said.

"And we'll make it up to you," Ralf said, "by taking you back to Earth."

"Tha' we will," Enry said. "As soon as we deliver a few things along the way. There's those Screen parts to Callisto, and that wonderful wine to—"

His last words were strangled as Shatz Abel tight-

ened his grip on the two pirates' tunics. Enry immediately said, "We'll take you 'ome ri' away, we will,
Your Majesty!"

"That's ri'! Ri' away!" his compatriot chimed in.

"And if you don't," Shatz Abel rumbled, looking
into each of their eyes before dropping them back
into their seats, "I'll feed you to each other."

"Ri'," Enry said, humbled.

"Ri'," Ralf added, rubbing at his chest.

Enry smiled weakly at Dalin: "Just li' old times,
eh, Your Majesty?"

Ralf said, looking up at Shatz Abel, "Yeah, we tol'
you tha' Shatz Abel was something, didn't we?"

Ten minutes later the ship's sensors went off
loudly, and the other three watched as Enry steered
them out of harm's way of a huge cubic structure
with a massive round port facing back toward Titan.

"Wha' in 'ell?" Ralf said. "Tha' wasn't there when
we came in, was it?"

"Was not!" Enry said. He gazed with the others as
the structure slid behind them; at its rear was a huge
cluster of rocket engines.

"Wha' was it?" Ralf said.

Off in the distance there was a flash of light, and
they looked to see a similar structure easing into
orbit around Titan; its engines flared off and it sat as
sphynxlike as the first. Beyond that there was a similar flash of light, and then the tiny flare of another.

"I know what those are," Shatz Abel said grimly.
"I heard some of Wrath-Pei's men talk about them.
And they weren't happy while they were talking."

The others looked at him expectantly.

"Well?" Dalin asked.

"How fast can you get us to Earth?" Shatz Abel asked Ralf.

"Abou'. . ." he shrugged, looking at Enry. "Three weeks?"

Enry nodded. "Ri'!"

"Well make it sooner," Shatz Abel said, his mouth tight. "Those were Martian plasma soldier generators being moved into orbit around Titan." Shatz Abel looked at the other three faces without a trace of a smile. "It looks like the war for Titan is about to begin."

21

"You tell me there are absolutely no problems?" the High Leader asked.

General Ramsden, the busy bridge of his ship visible behind him on the Screen, bowed. "None so far, High Leader. The first plasma soldier generators are in place; there has been no resistance as yet from Wrath-Pei."

"So Sam-Sei's new little cloaking devices worked, eh?"

"Apparently so, High Leader. We were able to completely circumvent Wrath-Pei's outpost defenses. And now the generator's inboard shields will be able to protect them until they are required—"

"They'll be required soon enough, Ramsden. You just do your job and make sure there are no problems."

"As you wish, High Leader."

"Out," the High Leader snapped, and the Screen went off.

If the High Leader had had a brow, it would have been furrowed now. So much going right, and yet—

And yet—

There was always problems and worries, but this

was an old one. He had had the feeling before, during the brief war with Venus and the plans leading up to it: the feeling that there was something else he was not paying heed to that he should. And here it was again, on the eve of this new battle—

And he didn't know what it meant.

So far, these feelings had proved groundless. With the successful insertion of the Machine Master's plasma soldier generators into Titan's orbit, he could begin to neutralize that moon at his leisure. And he would, as soon as—

"Damnation!"

He brought one powerful metal fist down on the nearest art object in the chamber—a sandstone sculpture dating from the earliest Martian colony period; he had seen the piece, a crimson representation of Ares, the ancient Earth god of war, in the Martian Grand Museum, and immediately ordered that it be brought to his quarters. Since then he had ignored it—except for now, when his tightened fingers crashed through it, knocking it into two separate pieces.

Idly he looked at what he had done; both the damage and the problem remained.

Tabrel Kris had not arrived.

"Pynthas!"

The High Leader knew Pynthas Rei was cowering on the other side of his chamber door—it was his customary position. After a moment the door opened and the toady entered, knees knocking.

"Come in, you fool. If I'd wanted to extinguish you I would have called you in before I did *that.*"

The High Leader pointed to the destroyed statue, which Pynthas looked at fearfully; the rate of his knee-knocking only increased.

"You w-w-want something, H-h-high Leader?"

"Of course I want something! I want to know where Tabrel Kris is!"

"Th-the life suit that arrived was empty, High L-leader."

"Stop stammering!"

"Y-y-yes, H-high—"

The cold quartz glare the High Leader turned on Pynthas, swiveling his metallic head nearly all the way around to stare at the toady, made the stutter instantly disappear, replaced by a squeak.

"Yes, High Leader!"

But already Cornelian had turned his attention inward, to his thoughts.

"Fascinating . . ." the High Leader mused. "She makes a pact with me, knowing that I won't keep my word, and therefore does not deliver what was promised, knowing that I will not dare attack Titan for fear of harming Tabrel Kris. Queen Clan, drug-addled though she is, is brighter than I surmised. And now she can*not* let the girl go free, because I will immediately destroy her homeworld." The High Leader's anger was lost in his attention to the problem. Almost idly he asked Pynthas, "And it is true that Wrath-Pei never arrived at Ganymede, as Queen Clan promised he would?"

"No, he did not," Pynthas said. "But our spies tell us that she did plan to fulfill that part of her bargain. It was Wrath-Pei who thwarted both you and the queen."

"Wrath-Pei . . ."

"Yes, High Leader."

"Alert Sam-Sei that I am coming to see him."

"Yes, High Leader!"

Still lost in contemplation, Prime Cornelian made his way down to the Machine Master's dungeon. He was momentarily startled on entering to find a young girl in residence; then, remembering that the Machine Master had taken the girl as a protégé, he fixed his gaze on her.

"You're the Venusian apprentice, aren't you?"

She was frightened, white as a sheet—and yet when she answered Cornelian her voice was steady and her eyes held more fascination than fear or repulsion.

"Yes."

Letting irritation jump into his voice, Cornelian said, "You will address me as High Leader."

"Yes, High Leader."

"Just because you work for Sam-Sei does not mean you can adopt his dangerous habits. The only reason he is alive is that he serves me. You would do well to remember that, since it also serves for you."

"Yes, High Leader." The girl bowed her head, but there was still that touch of defiance.

She bears watching, Cornelian thought.

"And your mentor?" the High Leader asked.

"He's . . ." The girl hesitated, and Prime Cornelian

turned around to see the Machine Master standing where he had not been a moment before.

Refusing to show astonishment, the High Leader said, "I understand you have something new for me, Sam-Sei?"

"Perhaps."

The High Leader waited for elaboration, which did not come.

"And it is?" the High Leader said.

The Machine Master said, "There is the matter of my long-postponed interview with Wrath-Pei."

Exploding in anger, Prime Cornelian shouted, "I have told you, he is not here! I hoped to have him by now, but once again he refuses to be caught!"

The girl had taken a step backward, but Sam-Sei stood his ground. "I was promised."

"And I have not broken my promise to you! *I do not have him!*"

Scuttling forward on his metallic limbs, the High Leader stood face-to-face with Sam-Sei. Still the Machine Master refused to move or blink, even as Prime Cornelian's anger mounted.

The face-off lasted for a half minute, and then the High Leader backed slightly away, hissing, "You are a good chess player, Sam-Sei; you have managed always to have something in reserve that I need. You know that I need you—but even with your talents, your usefulness to me may one day end." The hiss turned into a forced chuckle. "And it could be an abrupt end. For my part, I will turn Wrath-Pei over to you as soon as I have him. Now what do you have for me?"

The Machine Master fingered a slim device in his hand and disappeared.

In a moment he was back.

The High Leader said, a note of disappointment in his voice, "Another cloaking device?"

"Something more. I have been working on it for some time. With it, I can travel elsewhere and return."

Cornelian's interest began to heighten. "And so could, perhaps, an army?"

"Yes."

"And all of its supplies and weapons?"

"Of course."

"Excellent! And this device is ready to use? I am thinking of Titan." The High Leader kept his eye on Sam-Sei. "And Wrath-Pei."

The Machine Master said, "It will be ready soon. The range is not yet what I want it to be." He displayed the elegant device in his palm. "Young Visid here was instrumental in its design."

The High Leader turned to Visid with new interest. "So, we have a budding Machine Master here?"

"Perhaps," Sam-Sei said.

"Do I detect a note of . . . pride in your voice, Sam-Sei?" Cornelian said, his eyes still studying the girl, whose demeanor had returned to one of respectful bravado.

The High Leader rotated his head to face the Machine Master. "Hmmm?"

Sam-Sei, as unattractive as ever, showed for the first time since Cornelian had known him a trace of emotion.

"She is very helpful," Sam-Sei said.

"Yes . . ." The High Leader said. He made his way to the doorway, his metallic claws clicking on the sandstone floor. "Let me know as soon as your new weapon is ready, Sam-Sei. I can already think of some marvelous uses for it, and I have just begun to contemplate it. I'm sure it will be very useful."

On the way out, the High Leader revolved his head and fixed his gaze once more on the young girl, Visid—and noted that she met his gaze and calmly held it.

22

As he had with everything in his life, Porto made of his prison cell a stage.

He had mostly to use his imagination, since his body, once lithe and strong, capable of theatrical sword fights, leaps from mock roofs, and even dancing when required, was now nearly useless. Both legs had been broken during his torture sessions, and only one had healed straight; he had to fairly hop to get anywhere, and that only a recent development: before, crawling had been the transportation mode of choice. Most of his fingers had also been broken, viciously bent backward by Prime Minister Acron himself, who had also proven adept at beatings and, when in a fey mood, at burning various parts of the body with a hot iron or electronic instrument Porto had come to call the "Oucher."

At least there was pride, Porto thought to himself, in knowing that you've been tortured by the very best.

And so, his body stolen from him, he had taken to using his mind.

After the first few days since his breaking down,

he had let guilt overtake him; but, before too long, his sense of proportion and humor had returned. He knew there was nothing else he could have done, just as he knew that Erik would not in any way have blamed him. So how was he different now than he had been before? He was still Porto—Porto with a broken body and agonized mind, yes, but Porto nevertheless. So he had taken to dressing his cell—a concrete pit whose only window was on a level with the street outside; when it rained, the floor quickly became covered with rank water that took days to drain away—in stage colors, in his mind. To him, his cell became just another theater, with its own set. The water? A flood! The thumb-sized roaches on the walls? Ancient monsters, in need of slaying! His jailers? Costumed actors in his play, some villains, a few characters with a measure of pity for him and therefore heroes!

"Say, Raymond!" Porto called out brightly, knowing that his present guard, one of the better-tempered ones, could hear him, even though his words were somewhat slurred, given the number of teeth he had lost to the prime minister's fist.

Raymond grunted a laugh. "What do you want, you crazy actor?"

"Know what play I'm performing today? *Constancy for Constance!*"

The guard laughed again. "Never heard of it!"

"A Martian comedy, from the 2200s! Funny as anything!"

"Oh? Make me laugh, actor!" Raymond was brutish, but not cruel, and Porto sought to oblige him, raising himself painfully up on his elbows from his metal pallet resting on two-foot-high concrete blocks that served as his bed and kept him off the normally damp or wet floor.

"You've got to set the scene in your mind, Raymond!" Porto said brightly. "Imagine an aqueduct outside of Lowell, with a hole in it! Precious water is streaming out! A young girl, our heroine, named, believe it or not, Constance, walks by and puts her finger in the hole to stave the leak!"

As Porto spoke, his damp, chilly cell became that scene, and his voice brightened even more as he continued.

"Are you with me, Raymond?"

"Sure I'm with you, actor boy," Raymond laughed, "But when does it get *funny*?"

"Just listen! And *see* it in your mind!"

"I'm seeing it!"

"Good! Now what happens is, the aqueduct pipe begins to rotate, like they have to do on Mars to keep it evenly heated—you know what I mean?"

"Sure, sure, I've seen those pipes."

"Well, now our heroine, whose finger is still stuck in the pipe, has to go around with the pipe, crawl underneath, then climb up the other side, around and around!"

Raymond began to chuckle.

Porto continued, building the scene, "And now, just when she doesn't want to see him at all, Constance's *fiancé*, Bil-Bei, comes sauntering by, looking for her! And the thing of it is, Bil-Bei is from a very old Martian family—in fact, Bil-Bei's father is a

Martian senator, up for reelection—and any hint of scandal at all will sink the old man! So the thing is, Bil-Bei is out with a bunch of Screen reporters, who are supposed to do up a wonderful piece about Bil-Bei and his charming young fiancée, so prim and proper, and here she is whirling around a section of Martian aqueduct, dizzy as can be, looking drunk, with all these reporters taking pictures of her! So Bil-Bei just faints dead away!"

Raymond is guffawing, laughing out loud. "Hey, that's funny!"

"And there's all kinds of witty dialogue," Porto says, "like—"

It went suddenly quiet outside. The door to the cell opened, and Porto looked expectantly, but Raymond was not in the doorway.

It was Prime Minister Acron.

"I just wanted you to know," the prime minister said, striding into the room and bringing back his booted toe before giving Porto a vicious kick in the side, "that I am about to talk with Prime Cornelian, and I'm sure he's about to give me what I want." Acron bent down over the moaning actor and said, his face florid and red with vicious pleasure, "Within the hour, concussion bombs will be dropped on the heads of your friends and wipe them from the face of the Earth."

For good measure Acron gave Porto another kick and, breathing hard with satisfaction, marched from the room.

*   *   *

"Yes, High Leader!" the prime minister said soon after, into the Screen in his office. For the occasion he had scrubbed and brushed himself to military perfection, wearing his finest ribbon-bedecked uniform. As Cornelian's metal visage came onto the Screen, Acron stood at attention.

"Rather spiffy, aren't we?" the High Leader said. Acron, beginning to redden, couldn't tell if Cornelian was laughing or not.

"I wanted to look my best when—"

The High Leader held up a metal hand to silence the prime minister. "I've decided that your request finally meets my agenda. I'm in a position where I cannot let Earth problems bother me."

"Thank you, High Leader!"

"The bombing will start before long."

The Screen picture went blank, leaving Prime Minister Acron staring at his spic-and-span, at-attention image in reflection; after a moment he could not contain his joy.

"Finally!" he said, and marched to the window of his chamber to watch the show, which would blossom far to the west.

Hearing a commotion outside, Porto overcame the pain in his side and crawled across the damp floor. He stopped beneath the window and, wincing, hauled himself up onto his stiffened, ill-set leg. The pain in his side did not lessen, and he knew from its intensity that at least one rib had been fractured.

The cries outside his basement cell window became more intense. With a sinking heart, Porto

looked out, expecting to see citizens pointing to the
west, where Acron's bombs would fall; instead, the
few who stood on the street pointed east, which was
the direction in which Porto's window faced.

The sky was an ugly, dung-colored blot in that
direction.

"Raymond, what's happening?" Porto managed to
get out, between further flinches of pain.

There was no answer.

"Raymond!"

Now the street was filling with people.

Porto saw above their heads a rend in the still-clear
sky; a bolt of light shot downward, accompanied by
a shudder of man-made thunder.

The sky disappeared and, amid a sound like a huge
approaching machine, the ground began to rumble.

Outside, cries turned to screams.

And, as the rolling, flattening concussion neared
the Imperial Palace, and the jails in its basement,
Porto put his hands on the bars of the window and
began to laugh—even as the prime minister far up-
stairs began to shriek with the realization of his imminent demise.

Porto threw back his head and bellowed laughter,
even as the concussion reached and exterminated
him:

"Ha, ha! The final curtain, then!"

23

The garden of forever . . .

Roses, and a kiss, forever . . .

Slowly, ever so slowly, Tabrel Kris awoke.

And the longest of dreams slowly faded, like dew against the rising Sun.

For a moment, she thought perhaps she was merely within another dream. It had been so long since she had been able to touch reality that when reality finally did come, it seemed unreal to her. She lay unmoving, afraid to test her limbs, tired from the extent of her rest, and still not knowing, as the last tendrils of unreality loosened their grip upon her and melted away, if what she saw was real or not.

Where am I?

This, then, was a first test passed: if she could ask herself where she was, perhaps she was in a real place after all.

But what sort of place? If this was a dream, it was an imposed one: nothing in her own experience could have provided the building blocks for such an illusion.

She felt as if she were *within* something.

In the . . . belly of a beast?

Ever so carefully, she moved a finger; then another; then a hand and an arm. So far, reality held. She brought her hand up to her face and counted the fingers: five.

She moved a foot, a leg; everything worked.

She noticed that her hand still hung in front of her face.

Nearly weightless.

With a little effort, she sat up, and nearly rose all the way out of the open Life Suit she had reclined in. The locks, she noticed, had never been sealed, which meant that she had not been transported to this place within the suit.

Gaining strength now, she swung herself out of the suit and, eventually, landed on the floor.

It was only now that she saw how strange her surroundings were.

Like . . . an artificial Earth environment.

The tall ceiling was colored a deep blue; had, through illusion, the depth of a real Earth sky. Cumulus clouds moved across; and it was only when one looked to the "horizon" that the illusion broke: the line of the walls, where a projection of an Earth landscape was produced with false perspective, gave the game away. Beneath Tabrel's feet was a simulacrum of an earthly meadow; tall grass moved in an artificial breeze, but real soil held the faux grass stalks in place. There was even the faint odor of new-mown lawn—a rare enough smell on Mars, and one that Tabrel had relished on her trips to Earth.

There were daisies that looked real enough to

pick—and, indeed, as Tabrel reached down to pluck one from the meadow grass surrounding it, its own essence reached her nostrils and was as real as real could be.

"The daisies are real," a loud, imperious, gelid voice—a voice Tabrel knew well, that of Queen Kamath Clan—said.

Tabrel whirled around; the voice seemed to come from everywhere around her.

But now a Screen opened on one of the walls, destroying the illusion of distance and showing the queen's coldly imperious face.

How Tabrel hated that face.

"I am not Queen Clan, but an interactive simulacrum," the image said. "I am to tell you that you are in no immediate danger, though if you are coherently listening to this I have not been able to visit you for some time and renew your potions."

"To hell your potions!" Tabrel shouted at the Screen.

"I have no response to that; what I state is fact. You are presently hidden deep within Titan, near the Heating Core. The area you inhabit is nearly without gravity, for reasons having to do with the Heating Core's physics; these same physics provide, in the obverse, Titan's one-point-zero gravity at surface level—"

"How do I leave here?" Tabrel shouted.

The Queen Clan on the Screen said impassively, "Only I can provide you with entrance and exit. It would be quite useless for you to try, and only dam-

age to your environment can occur. You are quite
safe—"

"Screen off!" Tabrel said in fury, looking in vain
for something to throw at the simulated queen.

The Screen obeyed her instructions and ceased its
broadcast.

At the same moment, though, a second, smaller
Screen opened on the adjacent wall.

It showed a startling image: that of Kamath Clan
utterly changed, her physical appearance aged and
bent. Gone was the cold, sure cast of her eye, and
when she spoke, the imperious tone was absent, replaced by a harsh whisper.

"Tabrel Kris," the image said.

"Screen off!" Tabrel ordered, but the image remained and continued to speak. Tabrel ordered the
Screen to cease its broadcast and missed part of what
the Queen said; Tabrel realized then that this was
not an interactive image, but a mere recording.

"Screen, begin message again," Tabrel said, more
calmly.

Instantly the image returned to the beginning.

"Tabrel Kris," Queen Clan said, "if I speak to you
now, it is because things have not gone well for either of us. Please listen to me, for your safety and
the good of both our worlds may depend on it.

"The last two years have been, granted, a nightmare for you. It has been a nightmare for others,
as well."

For a moment the queen hesitated; amazing to Tabrel, who had seen this large woman as nothing but

a monster, it looked as though Kamath Clan was fighting to retain her composure.

"My . . . son, Jamal, has not fared well with the removal of Quog's essence. His . . . mind was not strong to begin with, as you know, and now, I am afraid, he has descended into something less than sanity." She tried to straighten her frame, which was bent like a broken reed, and somehow managed to look regal. "For my actions, I take responsibility, and, as you know, in the teachings of Moral Guidance there is always a reckoning for one's actions, good and otherwise.

"My reckoning will no doubt come to me, if it has not already."

In further astonishment, Tabrel saw something like a *smile* come to the queen's features.

"Along with my . . . physical deterioration has come, concurrently, an unclouding of my mind. And with it, I have formulated certain plans.

"We both come from great houses; it was my wish, and still is, that these houses be united. I live in hope that Jamal will regain his wits, and that you and he will be reunited. If you do not feel this way I understand, but that is still my wish.

"As you are aware, Prime Cornelian has sought . . . acquisition of you. This I have falsely promised him. In response, Prime Cornelian has sought to 'liberate' Titan from Wrath-Pei's presence. We both know what this means.

"At the moment, Tabrel, you are Titan's only source of hope. If Prime Cornelian believes that you are hidden on Titan, he will not dare to attack my homeland.

"In the meantime, Jamal and I have left our home-world, hoping that Wrath-Pei will be delivered into Prime Cornelian's hands; then my son and I will return to regain our place. However, if you are watching this, I fear other intrigues have intervened—"

"In*deed*!" another, cheerful, much more real voice interrupted.

Tabrel whirled around to face Wrath-Pei, who floated in his gyro chair at the opening of a lift tube that had appeared in one of the walls; it seemed to cut a hole in the far landscape, the breeze-blown continuation of the meadow which was projected there.

Lawrence stepped lightly from the lift tube behind Wrath-Pei, his stunted hands nudging the gyro chair forward.

"It took us *forever* to get down here!" Wrath-Pei chuckled. He made a dismissive motion at the queen's message, still playing on the far wall; Lawrence stepped forward, saying nothing, but a long line of lights and numbers flashed along the front of his visor and in a moment the Screen had blanked out.

"You really don't need to watch that nonsense," Wrath-Pei said. "It's a bit out of date. In fact, the queen is quite happy again, dreaming her dreams of Earth meadows as Quog's essence runs happily through her bloodstream. And still it took her days to get around to telling me about this little secret hideaway." His grin widened as his chair moved closer to Tabrel "Aren't you even going to say hello?"

Fighting the lightened gravity, Tabrel pushed her way past Wrath-Pei's gyro chair, thrusting Lawrence aside as she fled into the lift tube opening. Desperately, she activated the tube's mechanism—and, to her relief, the door closed and the lift began to rise.

"Hurry . . ." she whispered fiercely, willing the elevator to rise faster.

But suddenly it stopped and, with a gentle hiss, began to descend.

Even before the doors opened again she could hear Wrath-Pei chuckle, "Lawrence, you never cease to amaze me with what you can do!"

The doors opened, and Tabrel prepared herself to fight; perhaps she could pull Lawrence into the lift tube with her, disable his visor—

But before Tabrel could act, something happened within the room.

There was a blot of amorphous light that grew in the center, pushing a depression into the soil and twisting the faux grasses in a counterclockwise direction, pulling some of them from their bedded woven roots. An opaque, egg-shaped outline formed and then abruptly disappeared, leaving a man in its place.

Wrath-Pei stared at the new arrival, and a word caught in his suddenly dry voice.

"Y-you!"

"It is time for our interview," the new arrival said, with finality.

24

"Sam-Sei is *where*?" the High Leader asked, his anger tempered with incredulity.

"Gone, High Leader," Visid Sneaden replied.

The High Leader swiveled his head from one end of the Machine Master's dungeon laboratory to the other, as if expecting Sam-Sei to pop out at any moment. Then his gaze settled on the young girl. "And explain to me again: he has done what?"

The girl, the High Leader noted, had lost little of the composure he had noted in her before.

As if reciting from memory, Visid said, "The Machine Master concluded, after analyzation, that present circumstances would not lead him to his desired interview with Wrath-Pei. Therefore, he took matters into his own hands."

"Into his own hands . . ." The High Leader swiveled his head in wonder, then focused his head again on the girl. "And so he did what?"

"He has made use of the device we have been working on. A biofrequency homing device was integrated into the mechanism, which has allowed him to find Wrath-Pei and . . ."

"Yes?"

"In his words: 'interview' him."

"Simply amazing," the High Leader said, and without warning a chortle escaped from him. "And your part in all this?" he asked the girl.

"I helped him as needed, High Leader."

"Specifically?"

"There was much equipment to pack into a small space; I helped slim the device down to usable proportions. Also . . ."

"Yes?"

Stifling what was obviously pride in her own achievements, the girl answered, "I helped however I could, High Leader."

"Which means that without you, he would not have succeeded as quickly."

Despite the fact that the High Leader's voice promised possible rage, the girl replied, "Perhaps, High Leader."

"Remarkable." Turning the possibilities over in his mind, sudden realization of the wonderfulness of the moment blossoming in his thoughts, Cornelian asked, "And he will return here with Wrath-Pei?"

"He has no intention of returning here with Wrath-Pei, High Leader."

In the bowels of Titan, Wrath-Pei's voice was still dry. "Sam-Sei?" he croaked. "In the flesh?"

"Finally," the Machine Master said. "I have thought about this moment for a long time."

"I'm sure you have. . . ."

As Wrath-Pei made a motion to Lawrence, the Machine Master activated a second device, slimmer and smaller than the first, which he also held in his hand; the visor on Lawrence's helmet glowed a cherry-red color and the boy stood immobilized in place. Sam-Sei turned the device on the girl who stood staring wide-eyed by the room's lift tube opening; she collapsed gently to the ground as if asleep.

Wrath-Pei turned in horror from Lawrence.

"I have not harmed him, or the girl," Sam-Sei said. "But now we will be alone."

Attempting to rise from his chair, Wrath-Pei sat back down. On his face was a war of emotions; for the moment, he settled on cunning.

"Take the girl," he said. "She is Tabrel Kris. You know how badly Cornelian wants her. You'll be a *hero*, Sam-Sei!"

The Machine Master's horrid features showed no hint of comprehension; goggling eyes stared at Wrath-Pei's lionine face as if no one else in the universe existed.

Finally, Sam-Sei's lipless mouth spoke. "How many years has it been?"

"Not enough!" Wrath-Pei sought to smile, but failed. Desperately, he said, "I told you: take the girl and leave!"

"Until recently, I was not ready to see you, because I knew what would happen when we met again."

"Go back to Mars, damn you!"

"When I am finished—brother."

Sam-Sei advanced, and now Wrath-Pei, in a panic, pushed himself from the gyro chair, which floated harmlessly away from him; in the weakened gravity

Wrath-Pei seemed to float to the ground, his black-shod feet touching daintily.

"You were always so beautiful," Sam-Sei said. "So was I. . . ."

"Yes! You were beautiful. You're still beautiful! *I* made you beautiful!"

"You made me horrible," the Machine Master said. "From the earliest time, you could not stand my beauty. Only your own. You wanted to destroy any beauty but your own."

"You're right! Of course you're right! But there's nothing to be done about it now!"

Sam-Sei continued to advance on Wrath-Pei. "We were both so beautiful and bright. The twins. Gemini. Mirror images. Even mother called us mirror images. . . ."

"Yes, of course!"

Sam-Sei reached the gyro chair, still floating in space; as he passed it, he reached deftly into the chair's side holster and removed Wrath-Pei's shears.

"I remember these well, brother; I remember how you used them on me, after the Puppet Death you injected into me didn't do a good enough job for you. I remember what you did to me from the cradle onward. I remember the first *toy* you stole from me."

"I loved you!" Wrath-Pei pleaded, his slim, chair-atrophied frame backed against the room's wall, blocking the distant meadowed hill projected there; from far away came a slight, angry electrical hiss as Wrath-Pei interfered with the projection's normal operation.

"You loved no one," Sam-Sei said. "Not even yourself."

"Yes!"

Sam-Sei advanced, took his brother in a firm grip, and even as Wrath-Pei tensed for the thrust from the shears to come he said in wonder, staring at his brother's head, "There is a . . . spot on your ear that I missed clipping—"

The Machine Master dropped the shears, removed the first of his devices from his tunic, and activated it once.

Then again.

Still bearing the first device, Sam-Sei went to the girl and lifted her sleeping form, then activated the device once more. There was the same hum of light, the opaque egg-shaped shell surrounded them, turning now in a clockwise direction.

As they disappeared, Sam-Sei used the other device to awaken Lawrence; as they were gone from that place, the boy stood over Wrath-Pei, unmoving, data flowing across his visor madly as he looked uncomprehendingly down.

With Tabrel Kris in his arms, the Machine Master returned to his dungeon shop.

"Splendid!" the High Leader cried as the two figures materialized, and he clapped his two foremost hands together with delight. "More than splendid— you really have outdone yourself this time, Sam-Sei!"

The Machine Master gave the girl to Visid, who lay her down on the floor.

For a moment, doubt clouded the High Leader's voice: "She's not . . . dead, is she, Sam-Sei?"

"No," the Machine Master said evenly. "She can be awakened when needed."

"Again: splendid! I must . . . make arrangements immediately!"

"Yes," Sam-Sei said.

"And what of . . . Wrath-Pei?" the High Leader said hopefully.

"My interview with him has been completed," the Machine Master replied.

Pure delight filled the High Leader; for a moment he was in danger of embracing the Machine Master. "You will receive a medal for this, Sam-Sei! A new medal, the highest of honors—with my likeness on it!"

The Machine Master said nothing; already he had retreated to the nearest workbench and stood examining an open piece of machinery; only Visid, who stood nearby in attendance, noted the tremble in the Machine Master's fingers.

The High Leader, oblivious to everything but his plans, said, "And there will be a grand ceremony, Sam-Sei, at which you will be honored at my side." He nearly cackled with giddy happiness. "Because now nothing can stop us! Nothing! *This day we make war on Titan!*"

25

It was left to General Pron-Kel to make a defense.

He was not even a native of Titan; had fled Mars after Prime Cornelian's coup de'état, knowing that a purge of the Martian Marines was imminent and wishing to continue to live. He was also a Martian patriot, as well as a patrician, had lost two brothers in the bloody Martian Senate massacre, and lived for the day when Cornelian's metal carcass was hung like scrap iron at the front of the Senate chamber.

In his heart, he knew that this would not be that day; but still, he would put up a valiant fight with the Titanians, who were, by history and temperament, vicious opponents when attacked.

If the shields held, they had a chance. . . .

"Where is Wrath-Pei?" he shouted, not for the first time. If there was any hope at all of victory this day, Wrath-Pei, and especially his huge ship, which hovered at the moment uselessly over Huygens City, would be needed.

"Nowhere to be found, sir," Pron-Kel's adjutant, who he had appointed an hour before and whose name he could remember, reported. "But his protégé, Lawrence, has been found."

"Bring him to me immediately!" Pron-Kel growled, his mind already on ten other problems: the reports of activation of light soldier generators, so far repulsed by Titan's global shield; the possible breach of shield defenses to the north, which meant that plasma soldiers could be beamed down there at any time (thankfully, this turned out to be false); reports of panic in Huygens City itself, and in other, smaller towns—

"Here he is, sir!" the adjutant said, thrusting the repulsive, tiny form of the black-clad boy named Lawrence forward toward the general.

At any other time, Pron-Kel, out of a continued wish to live, would treat this boy with kid gloves; but now things were different.

"Where is your master?" the general snapped.

The boy said nothing. He seemed immobilized, lines of nonsensical data flowing across the front of his visor: "Ohhhhhhohhhhhohhhhhhh . . ."

The general took the boy by his stick-thin arms and shook him. A measure of pity went through him to see how damaged and frail the child was; it was like holding a bundle of twigs.

Suppressing his disgust, Pron-Kel knelt down to look straight into Lawrence's visor; he hoped the boy could sense his concern behind the data-spewing plastic shield that wrapped around his face.

"Where is your master?" the general said slowly, kindly.

The boy's ruined mouth tried to speak, but only

managed to make a sound and movement like a fish pulled from water.

Lawrence's visor went suddenly blank, startling Pron-Kel; the general could see the boy's terrified face in vague form through the semitranslucent screen.

Again the boy's mouth gurgled.

The word GONE scrolled across the boy's visor, in sudden large letters. There was a roll of nonsense symbols, and then an unbroken like of script: GONE-GONEGONEGONEGONEGONEGONEGONE . . .

Though he wanted to fling the boy away, the general willed his hand to pat Lawrence's shoulder and say, "There, son. We'll take care of you."

When Lawrence was taken away, Pron-Kel allowed his frustration to vent and hit his palm with an open hand.

"*Damnation*," he hissed.

In the deepest cellar of the palace, a room with a door that was never opened had been set aside. Behind that door Prince Jamal raved, still confined to his cage, eyes rolling and unfocused. His left hand, still attached to his left arm, the single remaining of his limbs, pulled him from bar to bar while he drooled and gibbered and laughed and spoke to himself, invisible others and sometimes himself: "And she's the *princess* she is, and what a *beautiful* princess she is! She's the *princess* she is . . ."

In another place, deep in the bowels of the planet, Jamal's mother, Queen Kamath Clan, had returned to Earth, far away from any sound but the warm push of spring breeze through tall fragrant grass; overhead, by the power of projection, her own warm sun shown upon her, and a single apple tree dappled the cloud-studded sky with pink blossoms that fell like petals of snow.

And, attached to her now in permanent symbiosis by a long red tube of pulsing flesh of his own devising, hanging like a grotesque bat from his trussing pole, Quog breathed from the queen's thoughts and mixed them with his own, strangely feeding on his own essence: and he lived again when he was a young man of handsome age and straight back, black hair and confident smile, before the Puppet Death turned him into an oozing creature, and when women including his wife found him handsome of feature and desirable.

A limpid smile spread across Quog's tallowed features:

I could dance . . .

In the middle of the Ruz Balib section of Huygens, a man made himself into . . . something else.

Trel Clan, fourth cousin to Jamal Clan, twentieth removed from the throne—outcast, layabout, unemployed, clever, calculating, and pensive—saw the future and determined to make it work for him. From the confines of his office where he did no work, in a bureau that had been created only to employ him, he closed the door and window. The room, already small by any standards, became oppressively so; now Trel Clan sought to make it even more so. He activated the shades, closing out the nondescript view, and locked the door against entry. Grunting with effort, for he was not a strong young man, he pushed a cabinet in front of the door, further ensuring privacy.

Then from his desk he drew with trembling fingers a kit of his own devising. For a year he had assembled the pieces; for the last six months he had quietly sought out advice—under the pretense of official business, for his was a department of such vagueness that any enterprise could be given purpose if that purpose was both obscure enough and surrounded by enough false paperwork to cause anyone with interest to quickly lose it—on the usage and application of each part of the kit.

In his facility with intrigue he was much like his Great Aunt Kamath, whom he had met once and from whom he felt so impossibly distant. But genes have a way of overcoming distance, and in certain ways he and the Queen were much alike.

Trel Clan was not only weak, but he was small—painfully so. (The pain had not only been psychic but physical, too: his school beatings had been legendary.) And he was not only small but cursed (so he had always thought) with the kind of hard, angular body that bespoke, rather than a frailty that might have saved him from beatings, a sort of jutting dare. His chin was sharp, his stare hard and resentful, his wiry hands often balled into hard fists. He had never won a fight, but always, to his misfortune, looked ready for the next. He weighed an inconsequential amount; and, when he sat down in a chair, often his feet did not touch the floor.

All of which had served him no useful purpose in life—until now.

Another of his qualities was that, once those he had dealt with had finished with him (either physically or psychically), they left him alone. He was ignored. In all of his years in the Ministry of Foreign Import Trade, Second-Class Division, Expendable Goods (MFITSCDEG), Trel Clan had never had a direct dealing with anyone else within the ministry. From the day he had arrived, five years before, with a writing instrument in his pocket and a meager lunch clutched in his wiry grip, he had never dealt personally with another denizen of another office either in his ministry or any other. Every transaction (what few there were) had been handled on Screen, where his dangling feet remained safely from view behind his desk. The single time that another worker had walked into his office it had been a mistake—and by the time Trel had looked up from his blotter the intruder had already mumbled an apology and the door was closing on his back.

Which served him well now.

Outside in the hallway, there was a kind of hive-like chaos ensuing, with comings and goings, whispers mingled with high voices of alarm. It had been such for most of the morning, since the announcement that a shield breach had been attempted by Prime Cornelian's forces—in other words, the war that everyone knew had been coming was here. The buzz had increased somewhat; Trel Clan knew that at some point, especially if a breach *was* effected, that

buzz would increase to a shrieking drone followed
by who knew what, and by then it might be too late.

So he drew out his carefully assembled kit now—
slim boxes, tiny cases, a pouch or two—and went to
work, ordering the Screen to become a mirror, which
it did, silvering immediately over.

It was also best to finish before power was lost to
the Screens; it would be difficult enough applying
the professional (only the best!), carefully assembled
parts with only a Screen mirror for help.

In a while, Trel Clan was finished, and stood before the mirror admiring his handiwork. Something
that did not often pass across his lips—a smile—told
him that he had done more than well.

He had done splendidly.

During the entire exercise his hands had neither
trembled nor balled into fists, but worked with a dex-
terity and loving precision that he didn't know he
possessed—another genetic gift from the faraway
queen.

"Perfect!" he said, and the smile stayed.

To General Pron-Kel's relief, the shields were
holding.

He had expected no less; one of the reasons he had
consented to take the job that had once been held
by General Tarn was the first-rate nature of Titan's
defenses. This would not be a walk-through for
Prime Cornelian, like Venus had been: and for two
reasons. First was the unbreakable nature of Titan's
shield. No one man could betray it; security had been
honed to an art on Titan.

The other reason Pron-Kel had taken the post was his unassailable belief in the fighting spirit of the Titanians themselves. Almost to a man they would battle to the death to defend their homeworld and their families. They all knew what was at stake; all knew that if Cornelian's plasma soldiers were able to reach the moon's surface they would be nearly unstoppable (though Titan's scientists had tried for years to devise an effective deterrent, they had been unsuccessful); and all knew, finally, that if Cornelian followed his Venus plan, what it meant for each and every Titanian.

But they were as ready as they would ever be—*and the shields were holding.*

"Every breach attempt has been repulsed, sir," Pron-Kel's second in command, the native Titanian and religious figure Solk said. Though she had had no formal military training, it had been obvious to Pron-Kel for some time that Solk would make an excellent second: she was respected worldwide, was one of the few of the religious sect not of Queen Clan's family, which made her valuable as a uniting force—and she just plain seemed to understand what had to be done. Pron-Kel's only reservation had been her age, ninety-three, but Solk had quickly dissipated that worry by pitching in to help move heavy equipment when the current command post, outside on the grounds of the palace under a huge tent, had been established.

"I expect no less," the general said, and by the twinkle in Solk's eyes he knew that she understood his bravado and recognized his relief.

To reassure him, she touched the sleeve of his tunic lightly and said, "They can hold indefinitely, General."

Holding her gaze, Pron-Kel said, "Do you think Cornelian will settle for a long siege?"

"We both know he will not. He is impatient and testy. He will either retreat or do something foolish."

The general said, "It's a shame that Wrath-Pei could not be made use of."

For a moment, Solk's face hardened. "It is not a shame that he is gone. And as for being useful to us, there is nothing in his past history to indicate that he would have been useful to anyone."

The general nodded.

Solk said, "But perhaps we should plan on using his ship as a possible lifeboat for the children, in case something unforeseen should happen? All of Wrath-Pei's men have more or less been incorporated into our own forces, and there would be no problem getting the ship piloted."

"I don't like that word: unforeseen," Pron-Kel said.

Again Solk touched the general's arm with two gentle fingers. "No one likes it," she said, smiling thinly. "But it is what we live by."

"Or die by," General Pron-Kel said.

Twelve hours later, at the end of the first long day of what General Pron-Kel figured to be many, an aide summoned him not ten minutes after his head had found his pillow, which had been a stranger to him lately.

"General, Commander Solk thinks you should come immediately."

Hauling himself with a grunt out of his bed and putting on a tunic, the general said, "The shields haven't been breached, have they?"

"No, sir," the aide said. "Not exactly."

The general cocked an eyebrow at the aide—who quickly added "I'm sorry, that's all I know, sir"—then quickly finished his dress and joined Commander Solk in the command center.

Studying a bank of Screens, Solk said, "Cornelian's plasma generators have disappeared."

Pron-Kel was filled with a thrill of hope, which he quickly calmed with rational thought. "Has he cloaked them again?"

"No. Now that we are aware of his cloaking device we would have been able to pick that up. They've been . . . removed."

"Removed? Could he have given up so soon?"

Solk said grimly, "It's more likely that this is one of those 'unforeseen circumstances' we spoke of."

"But what—" the general began.

"General Pron-Kel! Commander Solk!" came a frantic voice down the line of consoles. "The plasma generators are back—*inside our shields!*"

Solk turned back to her own Screen. "It's true," she said grimly. "Every one of the Martian plasma generators is now in low orbit—*below* our shields."

"That's impossible!" Pron-Kel said. "Our shields were never breached, were they?"

There was silence, and then another voice on another console said, "No, General. The shields have held steady."

"Can we move the shields closer, to shut out the generators again?" Pron-Kel said.

There was stony silence.

"*Can we?*" the general shouted.

"No, sir," a voice came.

Unable to hide a roar of rage, Pron-Kel strode out of the command tent; almost immediately, his eyes were blinded by shafts of light streaming down from the newly positioned plasma soldier generators.

Solk had joined him, her severe face upturned. When the general's eyes met hers, he tried unsuccessfully to hide his resignation.

"Get the children onto Wrath-Pei's ship," General Pron-Kel said quietly, then went back into the command tent to coordinate a last stand.

Waiting patiently by his desk, Trel Clan knew what was happening. His Screen was on, the sound off, but the shouts and cries outside in the ministry's hallway perfectly mimicked the Screen's action.

Occasionally a plasma soldier, a humanoid form made all of light, could be glimpsed on the Screen— soon after, that picture would go blank and another view would replace it. The outside wide-angle shots were spectacular: Titan's dark sky lit with light brighter than the daylight generators had ever produced—so bright that, for the first time in Trel Clan's life, he could not see the stars, only the radiant beams from the plasma soldier generators low in orbit. Then all of the beams went out as one, bringing back eerie darkness, permeated by the soft glow of plasma troop movements.

The close-in shots were more horrific—fierce close-in battles that ended with a blank Screen or a close-up remote-controlled shot of a pile of severed Titanian bodies, some with battle cries still locked on their dead lips and useless weapons clutched in dead hands. Trel Clan watched with interest as raser fire, whether at close quarters from a hand weapon or by rifle or cannon fire, went right through the light soldiers, impeding them not in the least. A stick of wood or metal rod used as defense seemed to bounce off the plasma bodies; such an attack was inevitably followed by a lightning-quick movement from the assaulted light soldier, resulting in a bisected human attacker, lifeblood pumping onto the ground. Waves of attacking Titanian soldiers were quickly reduced to dying piles of twitching bodies by as little as two or three plasma infantrymen; desperate measures, such as the spilling of hot liquids from rooftops, attempted rammings by vehicles, all met with failure. A group of enterprising young men managed to tilt a ground transport over onto two plasma soldiers; after a moment of seeming victory the light forms seemed to flash out from beneath the wreckage, regained their forms, and proceeded to destroy the young men in an instant.

In the Ministry of Foreign Import Trade, Second-Class Division, Expendable Goods (MFITSCDEG) hallway, the commotion was reaching crisis proportions; already the electricity had gone off and on, and what sounded like raser fire now punctuated the shouts and screams.

When the Screen finally did blink off for good, followed by a permanent loss of electricity, Trel Clan calmly lowered his feet to the floor from his chair and walked to the window; there he sat on the floor with his back against the wall and waited.

There came a tentative sound at his door; a voice vaguely familiar from the ministry shouted, "Doesn't anyone work in there?" When there came a reply from another vaguely familiar voice in the hallway of "Don't know," the first speaker grunted and the two moved on.

There were more shouts and more raser fire; then a short period of relative silence, at least in the hallway—battle sounds could still be heard outside the window, in a great general rumble of activity.

Then came the sound of marching out in the hallway; and the sound of other doors being opened one by one in a succession getting closer to Trel Clan's own; then finally his own was tried, and opened, leaving the intruders with the moved furniture to contend with.

Trel Clan readied himself, made himself look presentable and believable.

Two loud sounds, and the furniture was not so much moved as blasted aside.

Trel Clan faced his intruders; for a moment his heart sank, because they were not the plasma soldiers he had expected, but black-suited soldiers formerly in the employ of Wrath-Pei.

They shone a light around the room; it hit Trel Clan.

The soldier held the light steady, studying Trel Clan's hunched form, mock-frightened eyes, thumb in his mouth.

Finally the soldier barked, "Here's another child! Get him out of here, quick!"

In Huygens City, outside the palace, the perimeter defenses were shrinking. Two light soldiers had beamed down on the palace grounds, but they had been drawn out of the ring by a squadron of Titanian soldiers, subsequently slaughtered. One of the plasma generator's shields had been damaged, the satellite eventually destroyed by raser cannon fire; a platoon of light soldiers east of the city had immediately vanished, which had sent up a brief cry of victory from the Titanian defenders—until a new plasma generator had materialized in the old one's place and the platoon of plasma invaders had beamed down anew.

And then the western defenses began to crumble. General Pron-Kel, in his command tent, watched it happen on a Screen.

"Shore up that area!" he shouted, knowing full well that there was little to shore it up with. Already most of the technicians in the tent had been given weapons and sent out to do battle; only one other technician, and Commander Solk, remained in the tent.

"Wrath-Pei's ship?" the general asked, and Solk said quietly, "So far, it has not been touched. When it is filled, we will shut off the shields and it will make a run for it. That is all we can hope."

"We'll flank it with every ship we can find. It's obvious we're going to lose here on the ground."

Commander Solk turned her old eyes on the general and said quietly, even as the Screen before them showed a complete breach of the western defenses, "Yes."

It was time to leave Earth.

Something stirred within Queen Kamath Clan, and she responded to it. In her perpetual dream, the skies of Earth were clouding, darkening, and the petaled apple tree lost its petals in a sudden bracing gust of cold wind, which made Kamath shiver.

"Titan . . ." she mumbled.

Standing unsteadily, the queen tried to focus her eyes on her surroundings. She took a step, and the fleshy strip connecting her to the inverted Quog stayed her. She blinked and focused her eyes on the connector, watching the slow pulse of the liquid flowing toward her upper arm.

It was time to leave Earth.

She forced her eyes along the length of the flesh, which snaked back to Quog's chest.

"Quog . . ." the queen said dreamily.

The old man opened one deeply deformed eye, but made no sound but a rustle.

Time to leave Earth. . . .

"I must go to my Titan," Queen Clan said, and now Quog began to shiver, his mouth opening and closing soundlessly as the queen began to pull weakly at the flesh strip that led into her.

In the briefest of whispers, Quog said, "No . . . o . . . o . . ."

Upside down, the old man began to rock on his perch, holding out one deformed, puttylike hand in supplication.

"No . . . o . . . o . . ."

With a faint ripping sound, the flesh strip dropped from the queen's arm; for a moment she looked at it with incomprehension, her thoughts still caught by dreams of Earth and the smell of grass in her nostrils.

Time to leave Earth. . . .

The spot where the flesh strip had been was blue-black and swollen, puckered like a hungry mouth, slowly bleeding a mixture of blood and Quog's essence; the pucker tried to suck in the essence, but even now was closing.

The queen walked unsteadily to the lift tube's door.

"Open," she whispered, and it obeyed.

Quog, behind her, with failing strength, tried to reel in the length of pulsing flesh; but even in the middle of his labor he failed, his arms dropping like weights toward the floor, the flesh strip unreeling, pumping his drying essence tepidly out as the old man's eyes went glassy, their last vision the ruined queen moving slowly away.

He tried to hold a hand out toward her—even as his heart stopped beating.

*   *   *

After an eternity, Queen Clan emerged from the lift tube, stumbled through the corridors of the palace and outside into her realm.

How bright it was!

How filled with destruction!

With dreams of Earth fading in her memory, she came to realize what was happening and was filled with a sudden spasm of terror and rage.

"*Cornelian!*" she screamed.

From a nearby tent two figures emerged. She knew them; General Pron-Kel and Solk, the religious leader.

They hurried toward her tottering frame; but then came two flashes of light, and beside them suddenly stood two figures all made of light.

And then Pron-Kel and Solk lay ruined on the ground; behind them, a third Titanian, a young man, emerged from the tent, but he, too, was immediately cut down.

Around her, Queen Clan was suddenly ringed by soldiers of light; even as they converged and she felt them cut into her, she raised her fists to the over-bright heavens.

"*Damn you, Cornelian!*"

Memories of Earth and Titan dimmed and went out within her.

Titan's shields went down, which was the signal for Captain Stel-Far to gun his engines.

In a matter of moments, Wrath-Pei's huge ship was free of Titanian airspace; within a half hour, Captain Stel-Far had put enough distance between himself and the Saturnian moon to begin to breathe again. The plan was to make a run for the lower cloud tops of Saturn and remain there, hoping that the interference from the planet itself and its rings would enable them to avoid detection.

Then, in a few days . . .

"What in hellation—"

Suddenly Wrath-Pei's ship was surrounded by a phalanx of Martian cruisers. They had appeared out of nowhere, undetected, and now closed in to boarding speed.

Before Captain Stel-Far could even order his battle stations to fire on the hostile ships, one of the Martian cruisers activated a smaller version of one of the plasma generators in its snout; there was a bar of light that bathed Wrath-Pei's ship in light from stem to stern.

The captain, sensing movement behind him, turned in his seat to see a plasma solder leaning down over him.

He was able to give a strangled cry of protest before annihilation.

Settled in one of the ship's huge holds along with a hundred children, Trel Clan waited patiently. He had already rejected offers of friendship from two eleven-year-olds, who wanted him to play a card game with them: a brisk curse and dismissive wave of his hand had sent them on their way. Since that confrontation, hours ago, Trel Clan had been left alone to contemplate his empty belly; he wondered when they would be fed, and what kind of pablum it would be—

The hold's wide doors flew open; for a moment a knot of true terror replaced hunger in Trel Clan's stomach at the sight of six plasma soldiers marching into the room ahead of a Martian Marine. But he calmed himself, following the plan he had crafted so diligently these past months.

The plasma soldiers fanned out into the room, studying the children one by one.

Quickly Trel Clan sidled over to one of the children whose advances he had previously rejected; the boy held a clutch of playing cards loosely in his hand as he stared openmouthed at the nearest light soldier making its way in their direction.

"Here, let's play," Trel Clan said fiercely. Getting no reaction from the child, he hunched down and tried to imitate the child's demeanor, holding his own cards and looking with wonder up at the light soldier, who reached them, paused, and then moved on.

After the light soldiers had traversed the room and returned to flank the Martian Marine, the boy turned finally to Trel Clan and said, "Do you want to play now?"

"Later," Trel Clan snapped irritably, pushing the cards he held back into the boy's hand.

Trel Clan's eyes were on the Martian Marine, who now stepped boldly into the room, smiled a false smile, and proclaimed, "Children! I am proud to announce to you today that you are now happy subjects of the High Leader of Mars!"

26

In her solitary orbit amid debris, Kay Free continued to wait.

But no calling had come. Her own melancholy had once again deepened, to the point where she had moved from the Kuiper Belt to the much farther out and lonelier Oort Cloud. In the Oort Cloud were the ancients of this Solar System, bits of detritus from its very beginnings, the longest period comets, ice balls that took thousands of years to make their way toward the distant Sun. Sol itself was so far away that it was nearly lost in the stellar background, but the lack of warmth or brilliance only added to Kay Free's mood of despondency. She had begun to wonder if one were not feeding the other.

She had begun to wonder about much. . . .

"Kay Free?"

Startled, and angry at herself for not sensing another presence, Kay Free turned her attention to the newcomer; in the midst of her startlement she assumed it was Mel Sent.

It was not.

"Mother?"

Mother laughed, a bemused sound mingled with fondness. "You needn't sound so surprised, dear."

"But I thought you never—"

"Left my settling place? Ridiculous! You shouldn't listen to everything Mel Sent tells you about me, Kay Free."

Having regained her composure, but retaining her curiosity, Kay Free said, "Why . . ."

"Why did I come?"

"Yes."

"Simple: I thought you might be in need of some company about now."

Kay Free said nothing.

Again Mother laughed, and gave Kay Free something like a pat upon the head. "You know, dear, I'm not quite as ancient as you and the others think I am. And I *was* sent to oversee your progress. Which has been commendable—up to a point."

"Up to a point?"

Another laugh. "You're so *serious* all the time! I always knew you were the sensitive one of this group. And that I would have to talk to you alone eventually."

Kay Free found her questions and frustrations suddenly bubbling to the surface at this show of attention. "But everything we've done here—"

"Hush!" Mother said, though not sternly. "And merely listen. I will not be able to answer all your questions or soothe all your concerns. But I will be able to share my own thoughts with you. Believe it or not, I don't know much more about anything than you do. But I *have* been around longer. And I'm not quite the fussy and complaining biddy Mel Sent thinks I am!" Again the gentle laugh, and the pat on the head.

"I'm listening, Mother."

"Good. Then keep listening. Because it's what you do best. All I can tell you is that I was in a similar quandary once. And though I never did figure it out, I came at least to *understand* my ignorance."

"I don't—"

"Listen! For there is hope in this case. Mel Sent brought you my news of the young man, did she not?"

"Yes."

"Well, I am ignorant of why, but after brushing against him I am convinced that he is a . . . key to this situation. And I'm telling you now to be aware of him."

"Yes, Mother."

Mother gave something like a sigh. "I'm afraid that's all I can say, dear. These things are much more intuitive than those like Pel Front seem to think. And he's so *impatient*!"

"He is! And Mel Sent is—"

"Now, now!" Mother laughed again. "I didn't come here to gossip about your colleagues. You have a few annoying traits of your own, you know!"

Humbled, Kay Free said, "Yes, Mother."

Sounding suddenly tired, Mother said, "And it's time for me to return to my settling place. At least it's not so far from here." Something like a yawn escaped her, and she prepared to leave.

"Mother?" Kay Free asked.

"Yes, dear?" Mother replied, though her thoughts were already on returning, and sleep.

"May I ask you one question?"

Another yawn. "I suppose so, dear."

"You said that you were once in a situation similar to this?"

"Yes, I was."

"Did it work out for the best?"

"For the best? Don't things always work out for the best? That's part of the understanding I spoke of, dear." Mother began to move away; she was distracted now, her mind elsewhere.

"I mean," Kay Free called, "how did it work out for the . . . place involved?"

"Hmmm?" Mother said.

"The place where you were—how did it work out for them?"

"Oh," Mother said, a bit sadly, perhaps a bit of the understanding of her ignorance which she had spoken of creeping back into her memories, "unfortunately very badly, dear. Very badly."

27

The Machine Master, Visid noted, had been very silent all morning.

Visid was used to his silences, of which, of course, there were many. She was even cognizant of their differences. There was the silence of discovery, when Sam-Sei was so concentrated on a problem that the entire world was removed from his thoughts. There was the silence of frustration, when a problem would not yield to him and his concentration was broken by this frustration. During these times he would pace around the laboratory, obviously angry, and in need of anything but solace. In other words, he was to be left alone.

And then there had been a different sort of silence lately—which, Visid noted, was pointed in her direction; sometimes she would catch the Machine Master looking at her intently, with an unreadable expression on his ruined face. Rather than turn away in embarrassment when she caught him in this pose, he would seem to study her harder—as if trying to solve yet another problem.

But today's silence was different—frightening, almost—for the Machine Master, rather than stealing glances at Visid, had been absolutely avoiding her, to the point of retrieving his own parts and instruments and keeping a good distance between them.

Finally, Visid could take this behavior no longer and said, from across the room where she puttered at her own shop table, "Have I done something to displease you?"

The Machine Master said nothing, hunched as he was over an open hand transmitter unit (as he had been all morning, without doing anything to alter it in any way); but Visid was sure that he visibly flinched when she spoke.

"I said: have I done something to displease you?"

Slowly, the Machine Master looked up from his mock work and said, "Visid, come here."

The softness of the summons startled and frightened her; she was sure now that something was wrong.

The horrible thought struck her that she was no longer going to work for the Machine Master, that she was going to be sent back to the girl's dormitory—or worse, that the chancellor of the school would finally get his chance at her, to wipe her brain clean.

"What have I done?" she said, approaching the Machine Master one cautious step at a time. "Whatever it is, I'll work twice as hard!"

"You have not displeased me, Visid," the Machine Master said, and again the softness of his voice filled her with uneasiness.

"What is it, then? I'm not to be sent back to school, am I?"

"No."

The flood of relief that went through Visid was tempered by continued alarm. But still she would not avoid the direct question: "What is it, then?"

With something like quiet anguish, the Machine Master said, "I am to be . . . rid of you."

"Rid of me? What does that mean?"

The Machine Master was studying her more closely than he ever had—no, it was not that, Visid suddenly realized: it was that he could not say the words!

"Kill me? You've been ordered to kill me?"

For a moment the Machine Master did not speak, and then he said, turning to stare with his lidless eyes at the open hand transmitter, "Cornelian thinks you a threat."

"A threat to who?"

"To Mars. To himself. With Cornelian it makes no difference. He wanted to . . ."

Visid waited, tense with terror and concentration, until the Machine Master turned back to look at her; his eyes were pooled with tears.

"I told him I would do it," he said.

Visid, though her mouth was dry, said, looking at him directly, "Then do it."

"I . . . cannot."

Visid, tight-lipped, continued to stare at him.

"But I must tell Cornelian that I have carried out his wishes. So I must send you elsewhere."

"Where?"

"Venus."

A thrill went through Visid, and what had been a moment ago despair turned into hope. *"Venus?"*

"There is no one there, at the moment. You will easily be able to escape detection. And I will be able to tell Cornelian that I have . . . done as he wishes."

The Machine Master, despite delivering this reprieve, continued to stare at Visid with distress.

"What is it?" Visid asked.

After a moment, he turned once again to his work and said, "Nothing. Prepare for what must be done."

In a short while, Visid stood ready to be transported by the device that she and the Machine Master had perfected. Surrounded by a circle of her meager belongings: a few articles of clothing; a book of poems her father had given her and that the authorities had never, for some reason, confiscated—perhaps since much of the poetry within was Martian; a toothbrush; a bedroll. She waited for the Machine Master to activate his hand device, but Sam-Sei only continued to stare at her.

Finally, expecting that something needed to be said at this moment, Visid bowed her head and said, "Good-bye, Machine Master. And thank you."

Sam-Sei continued to gaze at her.

"You're not having second thoughts about carrying out the High Leader's wishes, are you?" Visid said, trying to joke but petrified that perhaps that was the case; for that matter, how did she know that the Machine Master had not lied to her, and that when he activated his device he would not merely scatter her molecules to oblivion or land her in the middle of planetless space, carrying out the High Leader's command?

Visid flinched when the Machine Master suddenly stepped forward and stiffly but softly kissed the top of her head. He pressed something into her hand, which Visid saw was a kit of delicate tools; but as she opened her mouth to thank him, he activated the hand device and the spinning egg of translucent light that typified the machine formed around her.

"Good-bye!" she said, though she knew he could not hear her words through the process.

The Machine Master, as ugly now as on the first day she had met him—yet somehow changed—raised an awkward hand in farewell.

And then Visid was gone—

—and elsewhere.

On . . . *Venus!*

It could be nowhere else. Childhood memories assaulted her; but it was, initially, the *smell* of the planet that flooded her with assurance that she was really on Venus. There was an open, wet smell so absent from dry Mars; an odor of sublime fertility, the promise of unlimited growth and fecundity. It smelled *alive.* And there was the wide-open sky, blue instead of pink, moist instead of bone-dry, filled with clouds that looked wet to the touch. It was so *different* from Mars.

Venus!

Visid could barely believe it. She had been transported to a small field beside a wide road; the road was dotted with the wreckage of war-blasted vehicles. A cluster of buildings lay nearby; some of them were ruins, but others looked intact. In the far distance was a mountain range, dominated by a volcanic cone; what looked like a huge glass spike was driven into its side near the summit, and a blanket of cloud rested over its peak like a crown.

Visid breathed the air: moist, not dry.

Venus.

She fell to her knees, overcome.

Home.

28

How could things get any better?

Prime Cornelian was nearly giddy with the situation. Things could not have gone better if he had scripted them out beforehand—which, of course, he had; but one never expects things to go *exactly* as planned.

Yet in this case they had!

How glorious!

And here, to be sitting at the top of the world—at the top of *Five* Worlds—it was almost too much to comprehend!

Three new comets—*his* comets—had even appeared in the sky to proclaim his grandeur!

How simply . . . magnificent!

The High Leader couldn't help it: he gave a little jig of happiness, concurrent with a chuckle of satisfaction—not caring that his actions could be seen by each of the two hundred thousand Martian citizens gathered before and below him in the newly renovated Olympic Stadium. The old one, though perfectly functional, only held a hundred thousand and had been built with *sporting events* (the High Leader

suppressed a shudder) in mind. Now that one end
had been blown out and lengthened, giving more of
a gallery effect, and the other end had been sculpted
so that one seat only, where thousands had been,
was highlighted (more of a throne, actually, set on a
magnificent pedestal of red quartz and surrounded
by a sheer wall of banners which flapped against the
sandstone wall)—well, now, *this* was a stadium!
Every seat, of course, each and every one of the two
hundred thousand, was canted toward that single
throne, which the High Leader, of course, occupied;
and now, in reaction to the High Leader's uncontrol-
lable act of happiness, each and every voice of those
two hundred thousand—as well as some of the other
millions who watched on Screens throughout the Five
Worlds, no doubt—rose in cheering frenzy, in shared
joy, with their High Leader!

Cornelian couldn't help it—he laughed, and stood
on his hind limbs, waving his four hands in benediction—while the sounds of ecstasy grew even louder!

There *were* minor annoyances, of course—there always were—and this supreme day was no exception.
Foremost among them was the Machine Master's failure, so far, to appear. After all, he had been granted
the ultimate honor of sharing the throne platform (he
would sit *behind* the throne, of course, on a low stool)
with the High Leader; and Cornelian was to make a
big show of bestowing on the Machine Master the
ultimate Martian commendation, the High Leader
Medal of Honor, the first of its kind, struck in plati-
num with a likeness (and a good one, too) of Cornelian himself on it in holographic relief. After all, Sam-

Sei had earned it; the reason Cornelian was sitting here now among all this adoration was the perfection of the Machine Master's transport device, which had allowed movement of the plasma soldier generators (another Machine Master marvel) inside Titan's defenses.

The least the man could do (besides making all those marvelous machines) was show up at his own presentation.

Ah! And now, here he was!

The Machine Master made his way, stone-faced, out onto the platform and stood mute. He looked so unhappy these days!

Oh, well—he must still be suffering from the unfortunate demise of his Venusian assistant.

The High Leader couldn't help it! He did his little dance again!

"Cheer up, Sam-Sei!" the High Leader said happily, pulling the Machine Master forward and presenting him to the crowd, which responded with glee. "When things settle down I'll get you a hundred Venusian assistants, if you wish. A thousand! Titanian ones if you want, too. It's just that there was something about that girl I didn't like. Or trust."

"I really must speak with you," Sam-Sei said, continuing to frown.

"I said cheer up! And here—take your medal!"

The High Leader made a great show of pinning the commendation on the Machine Master, presenting him to the crowd and letting Sam-Sei bask for a moment in their adoration before nudging him back behind the throne. The Machine Master, however, refused even to smile.

"I *must* speak with you,'" he said dourly.

"Later! First we must review the booty!"

And review they did, as spoils of the Titanian campaign were brought into the stadium and displayed lavishly before the crowd and the High Leader. There were art treasures, rare species of fowl and animal, foodstuffs that had rarely been seen on parched Mars: blue fish with pink gills, sea crabs a yard wide, and dilbras, a rare sweet fish that would be fattened on other delicate sea beasts before being cooked and consumed. There were antiques from the Titanian royal palace; gemstones from the Titanian treasury—sapphires thick as fists, diamonds that hurt the eyes, a ruby nearly the size of a goose—that had been well hidden in the Ruz Balib section of Huygens and now would nestle deep in the Martian exchequer instead.

Then there followed the children, who, after suitable study, would one day rule their former world in Mars's name!

As they streamed by below, the High Leader turned grinning to Sam-Sei and said, "There you go! Pick one out now! Pick out ten to assist you!"

Unheedful of the High Leader's words, the Machine Master said, "We must *speak*—"

Showing testiness, the High Leader turned away, saying, "Later!"

His spirits immediately rose again at the appearance below of a drawn cart at the end of the caravan, which bore what looked to be a large box covered with a rug.

Cornelian stood on his hind legs and laughed. "Bring it up!" he shouted. "Bring it up!"

Immediately, two attendants ran to do his bidding, lifting the box, still covered, and bearing it into a door in the wall below where a hidden lift would bear them and their burden up to the High Leader.

In a few moments they had arrived, setting the box down before Prime Cornelian, who laughed, pushing the rug aside, and seeming to reach down into the box, which was a hamper of sorts; he gave a cry of mock alarm and finally brought something up and out of the crate, holding it up for the crowd's inspection as a mother might hold a baby by its feet.

"I give you . . . the king of Titan!"

Jamal Clan gibbered and spat and laughed and drooled, suspended as he was by his single arm; his body twitched and his head jerked this way and that.

"All hail the king!" Cornelian laughed; and two hundred thousand voices joined in his laughter.

The Machine Master had risen from his stool and stood behind the High Leader. "We must speak now. About the comets!"

"Yes, the *comets!*" Prime Cornelian said heartily. He lowered Jamal Clan back into his basket and watched as the two attendants secured the latched top and covered it again with its rug.

"I command that we see my comets!" the High Leader shouted.

Instantly the stadium's lights were extinguished, covering the Olympic Stadium with a blanket of night. And there overhead, bunched together like brothers and sisters, were three new comets, brightening nightly, with growing tails.

The crowd ahhhed, and Cornelian said, "Glorious! They come to proclaim my rule!"

"That is what I must speak to you about," the Machine Master said; the High Leader was annoyed to see that the man had not regained his stool, and furthermore refused to look at the grand sight in the sky.

Peevishness finally overcoming his good humor, the High Leader rotated his head around to glare at the Machine Master.

"What is it, then? What is so important to you that you must interrupt these festivities—partly for your benefit, by the way!"

"The comets . . ." the Machine Master began. But now the High Leader saw that Sam-Sei was truly upset, not merely dour. For a moment a true bolt of alarm went through Cornelian, to see the Machine Master as he had never seen him before: frightened.

"What about them?" the High Leader snapped, if only to refuse to give in to fear himself.

"They will . . ." Sam-Sei began; but once again he was unable to continue.

"They will *what*?" the High Leader screamed, his voice echoing through the suddenly still Olympic Stadium.

"They are heading for our planet, all three of them," the Machine Master said. "And in nine months' time they will strike, and destroy, Mars."

29

One morning Dalin Shar awoke to find Earth filling his window.

He did not know how to react. At first he thought perhaps it was a dream—for the planet looked different, somehow, less . . . blue. He also thought it might be a dream because he couldn't believe that he was finally here.

Finally home.

"Believe it, Sire," Shatz Abel said, joining him as he gaped through one of the hold's picture windows. The pirate held out a huge hand and pointed at what Dalin thought was Afrasia. "You can see the blast marks where Cornelian dropped those newfangled bombs of his. There's no more Cairo, I'm afraid. Calcutta's gone, too. Wiped right off the planet."

As Dalin looked down in realization and shock, Shatz Abel's grim voice went on. "Looks like he dropped a bomb anywhere he had a question about." The pirate frowned, indicating a strip of bombarded area off the track of settled Afrasian territory. "I don't quite understand him doing away with part of the Lost Lands, though."

After a moment, Dalin said, "That's where my supporters would have been."

The pirate gave a long sigh. "I suppose it doesn't matter where we land, then."

"I should have been here with them," Dalin said, his voice filled with self-recrimination.

"Don't talk nonsense, Dalin. Did you have a choice in the matter?"

"Yes, in the beginning I did. I could have stayed. Instead of running away."

"You didn't run, boy. And if you'd stayed you would have died. And if you'd died you wouldn't be here now."

"To do what?" Dalin said angrily. "Crawl home to a ruined planet?" He glared down at the wreckage below. "There's nothing left to fight for! The fight's over—and I wasn't here!"

"Well . . ." Shatz Abel said.

"Halloo, Yer Majesty!" Enry called cheerfully from the hold's doorway. "There's someone on th' Screen for yer!"

"What?" Dalin asked.

Enry jerked a thumb toward the front of the ship. "On the line, Yer Majesty! Someone who don' b'lieve yer wif us!"

Dalin followed Enry to the front cabin, where Ralf was arguing with someone on the Screen.

"No, no! I tells you, mate, 'e's 'ere wif us now!"

Enry pushed Dalin in front of the Screen, where a man he did not recognize went silent, studying him.

"You say you're Dalin Shar, son of Sarat Shar, ruler of Earth?" the man said finally.

"I am," Dalin said. "And who are you?"

"Never mind," the man said. "If you follow our instructions, we'll clear this up soon enough. If you don't," he added, "we'll destroy your ship."

"Wha'!" Ralf cried.

"There are three raser cannons trained on you at the moment. If I tell them to fire, they will fire."

"Don' do that, mate!" Ralf beseeched. "We'll do as you say, we will!"

"I hope so," the man said. "Stay on this line for landing instructions."

Dalin looked at Enry and Ralf, and at Shatz Abel, who had entered the cabin and had monitored the conversation.

"We do as he says," Shatz Abel said, to which Enry shrugged and said, "Ri'!"

Twenty minutes later they were landing deep in the Lost Lands, in a part that was not even segregated on any map anymore. Through the ship's front window, Dalin watched the scorched ground rise up to meet them; it looked brown and barren, the only water they passed over a tepid line of yellow-looking river that fed into a sickly orange-brown lake. Dalin searched vainly for any sign of life, a village or encampment, but saw nothing at all indicative of life, animal or vegetable.

The ship touched down, and, as instructed, they waited, watching the sun sink into a hazy, smoggy horizon; by the time Sol disappeared, its color was that of sludge. The night did not so much rise around them as creep up above them; the sulfurous fog that

arose blocked out the stars and most of the surrounding scenery—in a way this was a blessing.
There were not even night noises to soothe them,
only an eerie moan of wind that rattled the dead
trees outside.

"This is creepy, mate," Ralf said.

"Yeah, I mean, no' even a bat or wolf to serenade
us!" Enry added.

"I don't like it myself," Shatz Abel said, his grip
constant on one of the ship's few hand rasers.

"If they'd wanted to blow us apart they would
have done it by now," Dalin said, trying to sound
positive.

"Then again," Enry said, peering into the muck
outside the front port, "they could still do it, I
suppose."

"Ri'!" Ralf added nervously. "Or wait till
morning."

"It looks like a long night ahead," Shatz Abel said.
"But they did tell us to wait. So we'll wait."

"No problem there, mate!" Ralf said. "No way you
gets me out into that eeriness, no wise."

"Ri'!" his friend said.

"Why don't we take shifts?" Dalin offered. "Say,
four hours?"

"Talk all you want about shifts," Shatz Abel said
seriously, his grip on his weapon tightening. "But I'll
stay awake all night anyway."

"Suit yourself, then," Dalin said, and settled himself down in one corner, with his arm for a pillow,
while the pirate continued to stare glumly through

the front port and Enry and Ralf settled down to a game of cards, cheating one another.

Dalin awoke with light in his eyes and Shatz Abel saying, "We've got visitors, Sire."

Stretching, the king stood up to see yellow fog floating four or five feet above the ground, and a contingent of feet marching below it, the upper bodies of the marchers hidden in the mist. Dalin counted at least a dozen figures.

Three came a loud knock on the hold of the ship; Enry looked to Shatz Abel, who nodded.

"Let them in," the pirate said, positioning himself to the side of the lock; Enry activated it and the lock opened to let in a foul stench and yellow roiling fog.

Too late, Shatz Abel realized that they had been gassed; he shouted "Down!" and fired out into the fog as he dropped to the deck.

Dalin dropped, too; but the gas was fast-acting and clung to the floor as well as the ceiling, and in a few moments Dalin was swooning toward unconsciousness and watched his three companions falter along with him.

He saw two sets of boots approach him, then nothing.

He awoke with a headache, aware of being under the influence of some sort of transportation.

When his wits had fairly cleared, he realized that he had been trussed and hung on a pole, like any hunter's catch. For a moment he thought of a deer or elk, and wondered if indeed they had fallen into the province of mutant hunters or, worse, cannibals. But a further clearing of his head as well as his vision brought his face into close proximity with that of a happy-looking young man, no more than twelve or thirteen, who was not, at least, dressed as any cannibal, but rather in a mishmash of military gear; his boots did not match but looked sturdy enough, and the cap he wore on his head was reminiscent of that worn by Dalin's own palace guards at one time: a tall, red, tasseled thing with a chin strap.

"Awake!" the boy cried with glee; Dalin now saw that the boy was one of four bearers of Dalin's pole, which was affixed with cross struts at either end.

"Thank God!" came a voice from the other side of the pole-bearing contraption. "Now he can walk on his own!"

Dalin was lowered to the ground and cut loose. In a moment he was being roughly helped to his feet and prodded along by something hard in his back, which on inspection turned out to be a raser rifle, borne by another smiling soldier, this one somewhat older than the first.

Behind their little caravan were three other bearing parties; Enry and Ralf were still borne, while Shatz Abel, surrounded by six unsmiling looking guards, plodded along, holding his head.

The soldier with the raser rifle prodded the king again. "Along you go, then," he said, and the march continued.

They were in country little different from that they had landed in; the ground underfoot was sparsely covered with dried grass and there was no life to speak of. The fog had dispersed; but the sky was not much more of a pleasant color, the Sun a wan yellow blot marking its path past noon. There was a faint, insidious odor like burned meat, and Dalin's mouth was unnaturally dry.

"May I have a drink of water?" he asked.

His four guards laughed. "Water? You must be joking."

"How 'bout a swim in the lake?" another asked, and again there was general levity.

"I take it you don't have fresh water," Dalin asked.

"Perhaps later," the young guard answered. "If the hunt is successful."

"You have people out hunting for water?" Dalin asked.

"Never you mind," the guard with the rifle said, prodding him onward.

They stopped, separated from the other groups, and rested while the Sun was still up. Dalin was given something that looked like a dried brown root; only when the others began to chew it voraciously did he sample it himself.

It proved to be dry on the outside but providing of moisture in the center; in a few moments Dalin was devouring it with appetite.

Only when he had finished it completely did he notice his four sentinels staring at him expectantly, with grins on their faces.

"Have I done something to make you laugh?" Dalin said.

The four broke out in laughter, and the one with the rifle said, "I'll say!"

"Feel anything . . . interesting?" the boy with the funny hat asked.

"Not really . . ." Dalin said, but then he did feel a rumbling in his belly.

Now he noticed that the others had not consumed their roots but only chewed on them, drawing out moisture, before spitting out the pieces.

"Oh, Lord," Dalin said, as his bowels flipped over.

One of his guards followed him a short ways off while he voided himself in relative privacy, while the others laughed uproariously.

"How . . . long will this . . . last?" Dalin gasped, between bouts.

"Not long. An hour or two."

Dalin said, "Next . . . time I'll just . . . chew . . ."

His companion laughed and said, "I'll bet you will at that."

There came a sudden far-off, deep-seated thudding sound; the guard's demeanor instantly turned wary and listening, his face tight and grim.

"What was that?" Dalin asked.

The thud was gone as quickly as it had come; and there was silence.

"Never mind," the guard said.

They resumed their march, with Dalin stopping the line every once in a while to relieve himself; eventually, though, the bouts lessened and, as promised, were gone in a couple of hours. When offered another root as they walked, he gladly accepted it but carefully avoided swallowing any of the pieces.

Darkness overcame them, and with it the sky cleared somewhat; they paused as another distant thud sounded, farther away than the first; and then, suddenly, they reached their destination.

Dalin was aware of abruptly being surrounded by a multitude. He heard before he saw them: a rustle that deepened as they walked on and eventually became a murmur of voices. In the darkness he could not make out his surroundings but deduced that they were a little lusher than what they had been traveling through; twice he bumped into foliage that did not splinter into decay at his touch but rather gave back with a springiness that indicated life. Then a single tent turned into a row of tents and then a city of tents; he was in a clearing circled by shanties and huts of semipermanent nature; a few fires burned beneath high lean-tos, which covered them and dissipated their smoke.

"Cornelian's satellites can pick up our fires if we don't hide them," said a voice that Dalin thought he knew. "Two of our other encampments were destroyed by concussion bombs when they got careless. By now, the ship you arrived in has been destroyed, also."

"We heard the hit an hour ago," Dalin's young guard reported.

"So did we."

From nearby, cries of dismay went up from Enry and Ralf.

A face drew near in the weak firelight, peered into Dalin's own.

"Yes, it's him," Erik proclaimed, quietly and firmly. "A bit older, a bit rougher around the edges, hopefully a bit more mature and without his eyelids—but yes, it's him."

Erik took his hand firmly, and looked into his eyes. "At least you're not wearing women's clothing as you were the last time we met." He smiled warmly. "Welcome home, Sire."

A great cheer went up nearby; it swelled and spread and Dalin was aware that he was in a very large encampment indeed.

Someone cried, "All hail to Dalin, King Shar, rightful heir to the throne of Sarat Shar and ruler of Earth!"

"Hail!" the mighty multitude shouted, in one gleeful, boisterous voice.

Twice more they repeated the cry.

Silence fell like an ax, and Dalin, nearly overcome with the reception, said quietly, "It's . . . good to be here. To be home."

Erik, still holding the king's hand in a firm grip, said, "We're bloodied but not beaten, Sire. The vermin Cornelian has desiccated most of the cities and many of our camps in the Lost Lands. We had to move farther in to avoid his bombs. He's destroyed his own puppet government in hopes of neutralizing Earth entirely." He let go of Dalin's hand and reached out to brush the king's eyes. "We have people who can do something about your eyes, make them whole again. It's clear you haven't escaped your own troubles, Sire."

"They're little enough compared to what your people must have gone through."

"*Your* people, King Dalin."

Shatz Abel made his way toward the duo and stood regarding Erik as if measuring him up.

Dalin introduced the pirate.

Taking Shatz Abel's grip, Erik said, "We know plenty about the legendary Shatz Abel. I hope he'll let us find room in our army for a leader like him."

Putting a beefy arm around the king's shoulder, the pirate said, "I'd be honored."

Overhead in the night there was a sliver of pock-marked Moon. Nearby, in the ecliptic, was an impossibly bright star, and below it, in the hazy, poisoned sky near the horizon, another of reddish cast.

"There they are," Erik said.

"Yes," Dalin said, and Shatz Abel's gaze, as well as that of Enry and Ralf and all of the thousands of others in the camp rose to the two beacons, so tiny in a sky full of stars, so large in their importance. Dalin looked at Mars, where his true love Tabrel Kris waited; and then he looked at Venus, the shining prize, a second Earth that would determine all their fates.

He looked at Shatz Abel—though his gaze took in all his people, all the people of Earth.

"That is where it ends," the king said.

Here's a Preview of *Return,*
Book Three of
The Five Worlds Saga

Ankus-Pel, a native Martian of the old school in politics, manners and breeding, thought that anything that did not bespeak Mars itself did not belong on Mars. He had never (so he boasted) tasted Earth food; neither had food from any of the other worlds passed his lips. Always, he had carefully inspected any item before buying it, insisting that its origin be Mars, of Martian hands. Once, on discovering that a certain piece of furniture, a table of beautiful light cedar (a reddish wood greatly prized on Mars and grown in the Noachis Terra region) had indeed been manufactured on Mars but had been assembled on Titan, he had returned to the shop where he had purchased it in a fury, his thin sharp face florid. Angrily, he had thrown the piece down at the store manager's feet, where it had splintered into wooden shards.

"You will not, Sir, fool me again!" he had fumed. "For you will no longer have my business!" He had then stalked out. The matter had dragged on for many years in various Martian courts, the store manager seeking payment, Ankus-Pel countering with nationalism. After the ascent of Prime Cornelian, the matter had been dropped by the store manager, and Ankus-Pel had gained his victory.

There had been many such victories, especially since the High Leader's ascendancy. Ankus-Pel's own son-in-law had been dragged away by the Red Police, and there were those in the family that whispered that Ankus-Pel had been the cause, due to the young man's unkind (and confidential) remarks about the nature of Cornelian's rule. After that there had been little discussion of politics around the old man, who eventually found himself estranged from family and friends.

But still his views had not changed; had, indeed, hardened to the point where he had divorced his wife, severed his relationship with his business partner, "A treasonous Martian if there ever was one," in Ankus-Pel's own accusatory words—though in this case the old man's indictment turned out to have little effect, since Ankus-Pel's partner proved to be more adept at politics (in the form of bribery) than Ankus-Pel himself, who relied on patriotism. Bribery, as is well known, will always win out in that contest, and Ankus-Pel found himself at the age of seventy with a lot of credits and a burning nationalism to sustain him.

And so he had moved to the famous Syrtis Retreat, with others of like mind, mostly old men with memories of long-past glory and dreams of future glory to come. Their retreat, a club of like-minded men and fewer women, was at least a magnificent place to reminisce. A former private reserve of two thousand hectares owned by the late Senator Own-Yei and ap-

propriated by Prime Cornelian, it had subsequently
been turned over to Ankus-Pel and his Fellows in
return for services rendered during the High Leader's consolidation. Also, in the High Leader's estima-
tion, it had been a way to consolidate these powerful,
rich, and rabid followers into one place where they
could be monitored. The two thousand acres, besides
containing the High Leader's monitoring equipment
(unknown to the members of the Elect, of course)
also housed a magnificent mansion of sandstone containing some forty bedrooms (fifteen utilized), a
game room containing a billiard table with brilliant
red top, a bar (much utilized), a Screen room with
seating for a hundred (again, employed by fifteen
individuals), a solarium, bath house, secret room containing pornographia (frequented by most if not all
of the fifteen), as well as planetarium, poolhouse, indoor tennis facilities, indoor barquis facilities (a game
for younger martians, which left this particular facility to the dust and sand bugs), as well as outdoor
tennis courts, barquis facilities and, for a reason no
one associated with the retreat since the demise of
the senator could explain, which meant that no one
could explain its presence, an outdoor baseball diamond: baseball being a sport which had never been
played on Mars since its independence.

But by far the most utilized facility in the Syrtis
Retreat was a room which had been added since the
Elect's establishment on the premises: the Historical
Room, which contained all of the artifacts of Mars's
current ascendancy and its bloodthirsty past.

There were relics in this museum room of the tor-

turer Ran-Kel, whose ruthless reign at the right hand
of Corvus-Mei, the Martian ruler during the early
years of the planet's war of independence with Earth,
had, until the rise of the High Leader, been long suppressed; here were his most prized instruments:
golden rods spiked with razor points, used for beatings; a whip made of sewn Earth-human skin; a ring
of human eyeballs in the shape of a crown, interlaced
with electronics to make the wearer think he was
wearing the crown within his own skull. There were
lesser exhibits of Martian cruelty; cruder instruments
of torture and mayhem fashioned by lesser artists
than Ran-Kel (if cruelty be deemed an art, which it
is not), as well as racks of weapons dating back to the
earliest made on Mars itself—but the most evident of
exhibits, and those taking the most room (three of
four walls) belonged to the especial atrocities of the
High Leader himself. Here, then, were all of Prime
Cornelian's special moments: the individual dismem-
berments, caught forever as Screen images; the fits of
pique ending in loss of life—and, most prominently,
the mass carnages resulting from the High Leader's
profound application of the theories and weapons of
the Machine Master of Mars, Sam-Sei.

Here were diagrams of the workings of the plasma
soldiers: their initial and subsequent campaigns; full
length holographic renderings, a rare (and covertly
shot) Screen video of the Machine Master at work,
complete with all of the genius tinkerer's mumblings
and profound silences.

It was all here, all the glories of Mars past and
present—and it was in this room, before dawn on

this day, that the Elect chose to have this most important of meetings, to talk of the Machine Master's latest invention, a gift from the High Leader himself.

Ankus-Pel, resplendent in crimson robes of the finest satin (sold to the Elect as Martian but, in fact, of Plutonian origin, by way of Titan, where the silk worms were bred), his thin, somber face topped by a miter of equally red hue, called the meeting to order.

His colleagues, less elegantly garbed according to their own taste and frugality (Ankus-Pel's miter was the only one in evidence, skull caps and bareheadedness predominating) were arranged around this historied room in their usual chairs, mostly of cordovan leather; beside each was a cherry wood side table bearing a glass of the finest Martian red wine, for the requisite toast, given tonight by Ankus-Pel in lugubrious sobriety:

"My Fellow Elect, it is a sad occasion we mark, when we are the only Martians of good faith—indeed the only of our great race left on all of Mars! I nevertheless give you," the old man intoned, raising his glass before him in benediction, "Mars—in all of its defiant glory!" There were no other words from the Elect; only a nodding of heads and a silent drinking of wine.

A robot attendant, whisper quiet, rolled from side table to side table, refilling glasses which were repeatedly and quickly emptied during the ensuing discussion of the Machine Master's Irregulator.

"Here, then, we, the Elect, make our stand," Ankus-Pel said, and now there were choruses of "Here, here," though not rousing ones.

Bal-Mei, oldest and perhaps most devoted of all the Elect, a former military woman whose career had been stained long ago with her involvement in a massacre of Titanian immigrants who had sought to establish Moral Guidance on Phobos (a stain which had been removed from her career by the High Leader) rose unsteadily to her feet; years, with the addition of wine, made her unsteady.

"I affirm this stand with every fiber of my being!" she shouted hoarsely. "I affirm all things Martian that make this so!"

A few more "Here, here's" followed, more robust.

"We all do, Fellow Bal-Mei," Ankus-Pel said; he waited politely for the older woman to be seated so that the meeting might commence (after all, time was short) but Bal-Mei seemed intent on continuing to stand; suddenly the old woman shot a leathery hand, finger-pointed, at the ceiling of the room.

"And it shall work! The High Leader will not allow it to end otherwise!"

Now another, and then another, of the wine-besotted Fellows rose from their chairs, pointing also at the ceiling.

"It will work!"

"I affirm this stand!"

"It is time to make use of the Machine Master's Irregulator!"

"Yes! It is time!"

Ankus-Pel, draining his own wine once more, found his own voice suddenly added to the others: fear and age making a wonderful partnership for action.

"Yes! It is time!" he said.

"Then let's be about it!" Bal-Mei said.

And so, this meeting of the Elect broke up not in sober Martian rectitude, but in, perhaps, a more fitting manner: in a wild scramble for the door of the museum room, which led amidst rose light to the broad stairway which in turn led eventually to the conservatory, a somber glass enclosure bathed in tea-colored glass-illumination, whose own, narrower stairway, stepped in thin slats of quartz, led upward, and upward still to the platform where once a telescope had eyed the heavens—but where now sat the Machine Master's Irregulator, a squat and wide tube of polished black, topped with an elegant bowl: as if waiting to catch something from the heavens.

The thing that filled the sky.

"No!" Ankus-Pel gasped, on seeing the horrid comet which subsumed the delicate pink atmosphere and burned white even now at dawn. At its flanks its twin brethren, sporting lurid tails, streaked the horizon at west and east.

Ankus-Pel's colleagues, the Martian Fellow Elect, cowered beside him. Three were still on the stairs, one below having already succumbed to heart failure; another staggered back, failed to find footing and tumbled down the quartz stairway to lie broken below.

"We . . . cannot stop it!" croaked Bal-Mei, whose own strength now failed her, after pushing past her younger Fellows with relish to reach the roof.

"The Machine Master will not fail us!" Ankus-Pel cried, thrusting himself forward to lay his hands upon the sleek Irregulator. "The High Leader himself, who is Mars, will not fail us!" On the platform they noticed the wind now: a howl which seemed to contain within it the wailing of the planet Mars; at all the horizons dust storms were swirling; to the North a huge, intensely red tornado furiously beat its funnel at the ground; while the sky, even in this early morning, began to darken while the comet above them brightened.

"Activate the machine!" Bal-Mei sobbed. For a moment she found her strength and thrust herself forward to stand at Ankus-Pel's side, her own wild face mirroring the younger man's.

"Activate it now!"

Ankus-Pel, half mad with terror, nodded and turned to fumble blindly at the controls set into the side of the Irregulator; as he did so his eyes wandered upward and then locked on the fiery rock that bore down on them all.

The Irregulator hummed, its ebony surface vibrated.

"It's working! It's working!" someone cried hopefully.

To the west and east there was a flash as the sky turned to fire.

The Irregulator shuddered, then split open, revealing . . . nothing within.

"No . . . !" Bal-Mei shrieked.

Ankus-Pel looked up with last sight to see the Irregulator's bowl reach to catch and cradle the monstrous thing above—which crushed and drove through it and filled everywhere at once.

THE POLITE HARMONY OF WORLDS

series by
VALERIE FREIREICH

BECOMING HUMAN

As a sub-human spy probe, August gathers intelligence from the inner corridors of the Harmony of Worlds' Grand Assembly. As a confidant and lover, he reports to the Electors—and holds their most intimate secrets. As a clone of a traitor, his days are numbered because of flare—a genengineered condition that always calls for termination. Now a catastrophe, which only August can avert, threatens to disrupt the Harmony of Worlds forever. But first he'll have to decide what to trust—his tarnished instincts or his growing hunger to become human.   (453964—$4.99)

"Impressive."—*New York Times Book Review*

TESTAMENT

Since the days of the slowships, every man and woman of the now quarantined planet could recall the memories of their female ancestors . . . every man except Gray Bridger. Bridger has spent his entire adult life trying to escape Testament, for he is that rare genetic throwback—a singleton, who holds no memories other than his own. But the powerful Bridger matriarchy has its own plans for Gray, a destiny that could crush his dreams . . . or make him the most important man on the planet.   (454596—$5.99)

"Compelling, original."—*Locus*

from ROC

ARBITER TALES
L. WARREN DOUGLAS

☐ **STEPWATER**

Old human, John Minder XXIII is the current Arbiter in a line stretching back to the early pioneers. But each Arbiter before him has held the ancient data blocks, key to all knowledge on the seven races of man ... and vital to activate the Arbiter's hidden warrior fleet.

(454685—$4.99)

☐ **THE WELLS OF PHYRE**

John Minder XXIII will find some unknowing assistance on the desert world of Phyre.   (454707—$5.50)

☐ **GLAICE**

As Arbiter of the Xarafeille Stream, John Minder XXIII must maintain peace. Now he must hunt far and wide for the remaining few data blocks, only to learn that some of the information he needs lies buried in the ice of a remote and forbidding planet called Glaice.

(454715—$5.50)

"Sweeping, completely original ... modern science fiction at its best."—Allan Cole

"Well-crafted and immaculately plotted."—Chris Bunch, co-author of *The Far Kingdoms*

from 🅡🅞🅒

*Prices slightly higher in Canada.
